Mills & Boon Classics

A chance to read and collect some of the best-loved novels from Mills & Boon – the world's largest publisher of romantic fiction.

Every month, four titles by favourite Mills & Boon authors will be re-published in the *Classics* series.

A list of other titles in the *Classics* series can be found at the end of this book.

GW00602615

Rebecca Stratton

BRIDE OF ROMANO

MILLS & BOON LIMITED
LONDON · TORONTO

First published 1973
Australian copyright 1980
Philippine copyright 1980
This edition 1980
© Rebecca Stratton 1973

ISBN 0 263 73395 5

Set in 11/13 pt. Linotype Baskerville

Made and printed in Great Britain by Richard Clay (The Chaucer Press) Ltd, Bungay, Suffolk

CHAPTER ONE

Dark men, Storm decided without hesitation, should always wear dazzlingly white shirts, especially when they were as tall, slim and attractive as the man on the quay. She had been watching him for several minutes now, ever since he had first caught her eye. Not openly, of course, but from behind the face-saving screen of a pair of dark glasses.

He was exactly what most English people think of as typically Italian. Olive-skinned, black-haired and with a kind of indolent self-confidence that amounted almost to arrogance. During the three days she had been in Bellabaia she had seen hundreds of people; men, women and children, all with that same colouring, smiling and good-natured people, but none as eye-catching as this man.

He was very good-looking, she could tell that much, even from her seat on a stone bench further along the quay. Tall and slim-hipped, he wore that dazzlingly white shirt open at the neck and further down enough to reveal the dark golden colour of his throat and chest.

He had a little boy with him, a small, rather sad-faced little boy he looked to Storm, although very much like the man, in a way, too. He appeared to be about five years old and was almost painfully thin, despite the healthy-looking tan he had.

The child was, at the moment, engrossed in the activities of the local fishermen, preparing their nets for the evening excursion after anchovy, and he seemed prepared to stay there indefinitely. The man, however, bent his head after a moment or two and said something to him, urging him that it was time to go, if the boy's vehemently shaking head was anything to judge by. Again the man spoke to him, and Storm, wise to the ways of children, either English or Italian, smiled to herself as she imagined the tussle of wills going on between the two of them.

The problem was solved a moment later, however, when the man lifted the boy and swung him up on to his shoulders, holding tight to the thin little arms while the child's legs dangled over his broad shoulders. There were no tears, but Storm heard the sound of laughter as she watched them, starting along the quay towards her, and she thought what an attractive pair they made, the man so tall and good-looking and the laughing child riding on his shoulders.

Although the boy was not pretty, there was a certain wistful charm about him that was much more appealing than mere prettiness, and she watched him with a faint smile as they came closer. Against the background of the little bay, with its incredibly blue water glistening like gold with the sun on its barely rippling surface, the little fishing boats bobbing gently and peacefully on the tide, and the

short, dark stone quay curving with the bay itself
and hewn from the sheer rock that rose sharply at
the far end, softened and bedecked with multi-
hued foliage right to its summit.

They looked so right, somehow, the man and the
boy, and the other brown, bright-faced people, so
much part of the scene that she felt a strange lilt of
unexpected joy at the picture they made. There
had been so much to see that gave her pleasure,
during the past three days, and somehow the man
and the boy had added their own contribution to
her enjoyment.

Bellabaia was a beautiful, picture-postcard little
place, with the rising cliffs soaring up from the
quay and the dark volcanic sands. Sheer cliffs that
had been terraced by these cheerful, industrious
people into a pattern of fertile shelves on which to
grow crops of oranges, lemons and almonds, apples
and pears. The scent of the lemon trees was everywhere and had even invaded her bedroom, in a
villa higher up the slope, where the soft wind carried all the scents and sounds.

It was a paradise she might never have discovered if a friend had not discovered it some years
ago and recommended it to her. Storm had decided
to take a holiday abroad before taking up another
post, and, as she had always liked the idea of Italy,
the recommendation of Bellabaia had been fortuitous. She was staying in the same villa, with the
same people her friend had known, and so far had
enjoyed every minute of her stay.

Being a children's nurse, she had a certain rapport with most children, and the sight of the little boy riding high on the man's shoulders made her smile as they came nearer to her. Their laughter was infectious and, as they drew level with her, they both looked at her in a kind of friendly conspiracy, inviting her to join in their fun, the child's eyes showing the uninhibited curiosity of the very young, the man's an undisguised appreciation of her as a woman.

She was a girl that most men looked at more than once, even in England, and since she had been in Bellabaia she had grown accustomed to being openly ogled by the expressive dark eyes of the male population.

Her tawny gold hair, of course, made her more noticeable in a place where every other woman was dark-eyed and black-haired, for tourists were few in Bellabaia, and her small oval face was more than just pretty. Even with her big green eyes concealed behind dark glasses she was undoubtedly a very attractive girl, and the Latin temperament was not slow to appreciate the fact.

Accustomed as she was to admiration, however, there was something about this man's dark-eyed scrutiny that gave her a swift and unexpected flutter of excitement in the region of her heart.

Her small neat figure showed to advantage in a bright yellow dress, sleeveless and low-necked, and the man must have noted everything about her, she thought, judging by the length and intensity of his scrutiny, appreciating everything from the top of her tawny head to the slim legs crossed one over the other and revealed to above the knee, where the yellow dress stopped short.

She felt almost bound to make some sort of greeting, in the circumstances, and she looked up at the child and smiled again. 'Good afternoon,' she said, but it was the man who answered her, and in excellent English.

His black head inclined politely, so that she felt sure he would have bowed if he had not had the child on his shoulders, and a warm glow of appreciation gleamed at her boldly. 'Good afternoon, *signorina*!' He had a warm, pleasantly deep voice, exactly the kind of voice she would have imagined him to have. 'You are enjoying the sunshine?'

Storm nodded agreement. 'Very much, thank you.' She felt a quite inexplicable sense of excitement again as she met the boldness of those dark eyes, despite the protection of dark glasses. A strange feeling of anticipation as she took closer stock of him.

'You are staying in Bellabaia for a holiday?'

He seemed intent on furthering the acquaintance, and Storm's common sense was warning her of all the things she had heard about the Latin male. Even the child was regarding her with boldly curious eyes, an expression strangely at odds with the waif-like features. Probably she was being rash speaking to them like this, but she could think of no reason for backing down now.

'For a little while,' she said. 'I'm between jobs, so I took the opportunity of seeing something of Italy.' She looked around her and smiled. 'It's very beautiful.'

'Very beautiful!' The expression in his eyes attributed the description to herself rather than the scene around them. 'You must allow me to show you something of the countryside while you are here, *signorina*.' One dark brow was raised discreetly. 'You are here alone?'

Wondering if she was doing the wise thing in admitting it, Storm nodded. 'Yes, I'm staying up there, at the Villa Lucia.'

'Ah, but how fortunate!' A raised hand praised heaven for such a fortuitous coincidence. 'We are at the Villa Romano, you know?' He looked as if he expected her to recognise it. 'You could say we are almost—how is it? Neighbours, *si*, neighbours. Permit me to introduce us, *signorina*.' He indicated the boy with a brief glance. 'This is Gino Targhese, and I am Paolo Giovanni Oliviero Veronese.'

He made the announcement with a certain flourish that almost drew a smile from her. She had thought the boy was his son, but obviously she was mistaken, if the names were anything to judge by.

Her heart was tapping away rapidly at her ribs and such a reaction was so unlike her usually cool and calm self that it surprised her. Possibly the idyllic setting of Bellabaia had something to do with it, but she found this man affecting her in the most extraordinary way. He held her hand for only as long as was courteous, but still managed to give her fingers a brief squeeze as he bobbed his head in a slight bow.

'I'm Storm Gavin.' Her pulses were doing strange and inexplicable things in response to that small but meaningful gesture.

'Storm?' He pronounced it as it had never sounded before, and raised a questioning brow. 'That is most unusual, is it not, *signorina*?'

'It's very unusual.' Storm pulled a wry face for the number of times she had been required to explain her odd christian name. 'But you see I was born during a particularly heavy thunderstorm.'

'Ah, *si*! *Una tempesta!*' The dark eyes looked at her in a way that set all sorts of wild ideas spinning around in her brain. 'It is very beautiful,' he decreed softly. 'It is almost worthy of your own beauty, *signorina*!'

Storm was unsure whether or not she should respond to the quite outrageous glint in his eyes, but instead she merely smiled. Paolo Veronese, from the speed with which he became familiar, needed little encouragement from anyone, but he was quite the most devastating man she had ever met and she could quite easily make a complete fool of herself if she was not very careful.

The boy, Gino, said something in Italian, and Paolo Veronese shook his head, smiling apologetically at her. 'I am sorry, *signorina*, we should speak English.'

'But why?' Storm asked with a smile. 'I don't mind in the least!'

He made a wry face, his brows raised. 'Ah, but Alexei *would* mind. When we are in the company of English people, he prefers that we speak English at all times, especially Gino. It is for his own good, you see, for when he is older. Alexei himself speaks it perfectly and he would have Gino as perfect.'

Storm nodded, looking much wiser than indeed she was. Whoever Alexei was, obviously he was someone whose word counted for much. 'Oh, I see,' was all she said.

It must have been fairly obvious that she had no idea what he was talking about, but Paolo Veronese had evidently meant her to be impressed. 'Signor Alexei Romano is Gino's guardian, *signorina*!'

Somehow the name of Romano struck her as familiar, but it took her a minute or two to wonder why. Then she remembered that she had heard her host at the villa mention the name in connection with an electronics firm in nearby Naples. She seemed to remember also that there had been some comment on the fact that he must be one of the wealthiest men in Italy. Presumably Paolo Veronese was an employee of some sort, although possibly a privileged one if he was entrusted with the care of the boy.

'Well, I can understand the idea, of course,' Storm said with a smile. 'A second language is always an asset, but this little chap is rather small to be bi-lingual as yet!'

Expressive Latin shoulders spoke volumes. 'Alas,' he said, 'Alexei does not always understand and Gino is sometimes——' Another shrug. 'He uses Italian words when he cannot think of the English one.'

'But what more natural?' Storm sympathised, and the warm, liquid brown eyes glowed darkly.

'You are so very *simpatica, signorina*, but——' Again those expressive shoulders said a good deal more than words could have done. 'Unfortunately Alexei sometimes loses patience.'

'Oh, but that's most unfair!' Storm protested without hesitation, seeing the child's side of it, as always. 'He must be an awful bully!'

She had not thought before she spoke and realised suddenly that she was speaking to a complete stranger about his employer. However, Paolo Veronese looked no more than vaguely uneasy. 'Please do not allow me to mislead you, *signorina*! They are very fond of one another, but Alexei is—firm, you understand?'

'I think so.' Storm still thought that anyone who could lose patience with a wistful little waif like Gino Targhese merely because he occasionally lapsed into his own tongue must almost certainly be a bully, and she wished she could have five minutes alone with the man. She would tell him exactly what she thought of him.

Paolo Veronese's dark eyes were regarding her again with blatant admiration, and he smiled at her warmly. 'How long are you to stay in Bellabaia, *signorina?*' he asked, soft-voiced, and Storm felt her heart turn somersaults again at the effect of that voice. It was really quite ridiculous for her to be blushing like a schoolgirl just because a strange man looked at her with eyes that made her think of all sorts of incredible things, and spoke to her in a voice that sent shivers of pleasure through her.

'Oh, only two weeks,' she said, pulling a rueful face. 'Then I have to go back and find another post. I'm a children's nurse,' she added, anticipating the question.

'You are?' He seemed quite inordinately pleased about that for some reason, and his dark eyes glowed. 'But that is *molto bene, signorina!*'

His enthusiasm puzzled her rather, but she smiled and nodded.

'I think so,' she said. 'I enjoy it.'

'*Bene!*' He glanced at his wristwatch and pulled a face. 'I think we must go, *signorina*, but if I may, I would like to see you again. *Si?*'

'That would be very nice.' She smiled at them both. 'Goodbye, Signor Veronese.'

She gave an involuntary gasp when her left hand was raised and his lips pressed warmly on her fingers. '*Addio, signorina.* We will meet again!'

Storm sat there for some time after they had gone, watching the activity on the quay, where the fishermen worked and chattered incessantly among themselves, their laughter and lyrical Italian voices carrying on the warm, sunny air. Air cooled and freshened by the soft breeze off the water.

Most of the houses were the little cottages of the fishermen and their families, or the workers from the terraced fields above on the cliff face, but there were one or two larger villas, like the one where Storm herself was staying, perched higher up among the fertile terraces. They were accessible only by steep, narrow roads that rose like dusty snakes among the trees and bushes, to join the main road out to Naples itself, accessible from the quay only on foot up the even steeper paths with steps cut into them and protected by low walls.

She watched the man and the little boy again as they began to climb one of the paths, the boy holding on to the man's hand as they went up the steep incline. A white villa stood fairly high up, brightly white against the tree-layered cliff side, like a child's toy. Bright yellow mimosa and scarlet geraniums caught her eye, making splashes of vivid colour where the gardens closed around the villa, as if to keep the more mundane crops at bay.

Another glance at her watch and Storm got lazily to her feet. The warm, sea-cooled air made her feel incredibly lazy and she marvelled at the seemingly boundless energy of the local people, who seemed to stop their frenetic round of activity only for the long midday *siesta*.

They always had a cheerful word for her too, and cries of *'Buon giorno, signorina!'* followed her along the quay.

Bright, friendly but curious eyes noted her passing, and smiles appreciated the picture she made, but it struck her today that perhaps there was more than the usual mild curiosity in the looks she received. Although she tried to dismiss it as unlikely, she could not help wondering if her short conversation with Paolo Veronese had been the cause of speculation.

The climb up to the villa was hot and tiring, but it was well worth it for the view from the villa's garden. Away from the quay it was quieter and a little less hot, for the higher one went the more effective that breeze became, and the scent of the lemon trees began to titillate her nostrils as she climbed.

Below her the quay, with its bobbing boats and cluster of little houses, looked like something on a picture postcard, and, as she paused part way up the steep path, from somewhere below a joyous, if less than perfect, tenor voice gave out with the strains of an Italian love song.

Anywhere else Storm would have felt the situation artificial and contrived, but here in Bellabaia it seemed a perfectly natural thing to happen, although the whole thing reminded her of something out of a Hollywood film. The sound of the voice singing, the sheer beauty of the scene above and below her, made her feel like laughing suddenly with uninhibited enjoyment, and she ran a few feet up the steep path without even noticing the effort it required to do so.

It was her host who answered the telephone the

following morning, while Storm was still having her breakfast, and she frowned curiously when he called her into the hall to take the call. He too looked at her curiously as he handed her the receiver, one hand over the mouthpiece.

'Someone is speaking on behalf of Signor Alexei Romano, *signorina*,' he told her, and Storm took the instrument from him with a sudden flutter of apprehension, wondering what on earth it could possibly mean.

'Hello,' she said cautiously. 'This is Storm Gavin.'

The voice at the other end spoke excellent English, but it was less seductively low in pitch than she remembered Paolo Veronese's. 'I am speaking for Signor Romano,' the caller informed her and, as Paolo Veronese had done, sounded as if he expected her to be impressed by the name. 'This is his secretary.'

'Signor Romano?' It occurred to her suddenly that perhaps the great man himself had heard about her encounter with Paolo Veronese and his ward yesterday, and was going to put her firmly in her place.

Further enquiries of her host had produced the information that Alexei Romano not only owned the biggest electronics company in Italy, but was also the last of an ancient and very aristocratic family. There was also something else about the name that struck her as familiar, but she could not for the moment call it to mind. But surely no man could be so autocratic as to object to a perfectly ordinary encounter, even if he was a business tycoon and an aristocrat.

'Signor Romano wishes to speak with you, Signorina Gavin,' the smooth voice informed her. 'Will you please call at the Villa Romano this morning at ten-thirty.'

It was not a request, Storm recognised with sudden anger, it was more in the nature of a command, and she was very tempted to hang up there and then. But then she remembered how, yesterday, she had wished for five minutes alone with Signor Alexei Romano, to tell him exactly what she thought of him. It seemed he not only bullied little children, but also issued orders to complete strangers, and expected to be obeyed.

'First I'd like to know why I'm expected to call and see Signor Romano,' she told the waiting secretary, and she could visualise the shocked expression on his face from the silence that followed. 'Why does he want to see me?'

'Signor Romano instructed me to make the call,' she was informed stiffly. 'No doubt the *signore*'s reasons will be made plain when you arrive, *signorina*.'

No doubt, Storm thought, her brain whirling busily, but she did not intend allowing herself to be bulldozed into obeying the summons without question. 'I'm not at all sure that I understand,' she told the man at the other end coolly. 'However, if I find that I have no other engagement for ten-thirty this morning, I'll call. If not, please offer Signor Romano my apologies. Good morning.'

She hung up hastily and turned to face her host, who had come into the hall again in time to catch her last words. His dark, friendly face looked quite stunned, and Storm wondered how on earth Alexei Romano, whoever he might be, could invoke such awe.

She was curious to see what kind of a man it was who bullied little boys and issued orders to complete strangers, via his secretary. He was probably some crabby old man with more money than he knew what to do with, and enjoyed making everyone jump every time he cracked the whip. Well, she would go, out of sheer curiosity, but she would go in her own good time.

Storm finished her breakfast and took her time over dressing, eventually picking on a simple pale green nylon jersey dress with long full sleeves and shirt-style neckline that offered a tantalising glimpse of lightly tanned skin as far as the shadowy vee just above the top button.

She brushed her tawny hair until it shone like burnished bronze, and the total effect, she decided with satisfaction, was cool and uncluttered enough to impress anyone with her complete disregard for Signor Alexei Romano's opinion.

It occurred to her briefly, as she started out, that to go alone would create something of a wrong impression on an autocratic and traditional Italian, but there was no one she could ask to go with her, and anyway, his opinion did not concern her in the least.

It was almost an hour later than the appointed time as she walked along the road and approached the Villa Romano from the front. It would have been much too informal to have come in from the path up from the quay. She wished she felt less nervous, but she was determined to hold her own, no matter what happened, or why Alexei Romano had commanded her presence. Despite her vow, however, her hands were actually trembling when she turned into a tree-lined approach to the old villa, and a heavily beating heart put unaccustomed colour into her cheeks.

The villa looked old and mellow and rather beautiful, its white walls dappled with the shadows of trees that surrounded it and gave fragrance as well as welcome shade. The garden was a riot of colour with the dark, stern straightness of cypress trees lending a background of contrast to the scarlet and pink of geraniums, bright sun-yellow mimosa and roses of every hue.

A long veranda ran the full width of the house, its tiled floor half covered with stone urns overrunning with flowers that scented the still, warm air. The door was ajar, she could see when she got closer, and she hesitated briefly, her heart thumping heavily again as she reached for the bell pull.

The man who answered her ring seemed to be expecting her, although his dark, rather dour face gave little away as he bade her enter, and led the way across the hall.

The hall was a revelation to her, quite beautiful and quite unexpected. It was wide and cool and its walls were covered in the most beautiful frescoes in soft, light colours and exquisite workmanship. Scenes of gods and goddesses amid scenery even more breathtaking than that outside. Slender nymphs and exquisitely beautiful young men who reminded her uneasily of Paolo Veronese as they looked down at her from their painted paradise with limpid dark eyes.

Potted palms swept ceiling-high, the floor beneath her feet was tiled with soft coloured mosaics, and to the right a beautiful marble staircase swept upwards to what looked like a gallery that disappeared on either side into shadowy coolness. She could, she thought, be forgiven for believing she had suddenly been transported back in time some two or three hundred years.

The manservant made his stately way across the hall and Storm was shown into a huge, high-ceilinged room, light and cool as the hall had been, and hung with portraits of dark, aristocratic-looking men and vaguely hostile-looking women, some of them quite beautiful, despite their discouraging expressions.

She was instructed to be seated, in much less perfect English than she had encountered so far, and the tall double doors were closed behind her. Left to her own devices with only the loud ticking of a

21

clock to distract her, she looked around her curiously.

The villa was much bigger than she had realised from seeing it from below on the quay, a good deal larger than the Villa Lucia, which was only to be expected. If she had not been so uneasy she would have walked about the room and admired the beautiful white marble mantel and the many expensive and beautiful *objets d'art*, but she found herself constantly listening for approaching footsteps and instead stayed where she was in a chair near the window.

There was no sound to be heard but the occasional hum of a car passing on the motorway above, and nearly ten minutes after her arrival Storm was still waiting. She was becoming more and more angry at the cavalier treatment she was receiving, but it did not take much intelligence to guess that Signor Alexei Romano intended teaching her a lesson in punctuality. She had kept him waiting, so now she was being made to wait in her turn, for him to put in an appearance.

Since it had been at his instigation that she was there at all, however, Storm saw no reason why she should be treated so, and she got to her feet at last, picking up her handbag and clutching it tightly in both hands, her eyes bright and angrily green. If Signor Romano wanted to see her so badly, he could come and find her. She was not going to wait for him any longer.

CHAPTER TWO

STORM reached the double doors and her hands were already on the ornate brass knobs when they were suddenly twisted out of her grasp and she stepped back hastily to avoid colliding with the edges of the doors.

The man who confronted her, she supposed after one brief, startled glance, was the secretary she had spoken to on the telephone, and she wondered vaguely if all Romano's staff were so devastatingly attractive.

This man was even taller than Paolo Veronese and less good-looking, but he had a fierce, almost animal magnetism that struck her like a blow. He was much less typically Italian too, although she supposed there must be variations in Italians, as in any other race.

His features looked as if they had been carved out of bronze. A square chin, deeply cleft, and high Slavonic-looking cheekbones that added drama to a face at once discouraging and incredibly attractive. His mouth was wide and straight and at the moment set firm as if he was angry.

Hair that was not quite black grew thick and strong and quite low down in his neck, a heavy swathe of it lying across his broad brow. His bearing was proud and arrogant and he emanated self-confidence, but undoubtedly the most arresting thing about him was his eyes.

Whereas Paolo Veronese had the dark eyes that one expected of his race, this man's eyes were a light, almost icy blue. Such a contrast in the deeply tanned face drew immediate attention, and Storm suspected that he was well aware of the effect they had, for one corner of that wide mouth tilted briefly and unexpectedly, as if he smiled to himself.

She would not have thought the terrain around Bellabaia suitable for horse-riding, although there was a racecourse in Naples, but obviously this man had been riding, or at least he was dressed for it.

He wore fawn breeches and highly polished brown boots, with a fine white silk shirt whose texture was such that it was obvious he wore nothing under it. The crop he carried he flung away from him into a chair as he came into the room, and he looked at Storm with blatant and speculative curiosity.

'Miss Gavin?'

It was not the man on the telephone, she had already decided that, for apart from the unlikelihood of a secretary receiving her dressed as he was, his voice was deeper and more resonant, and he gave the impression that he would never serve anyone, in any capacity.

She nodded uncertainly, her heart in her throat suddenly when she began to suspect his identity. 'I'm Storm Gavin,' she admitted.

He cast a swift, exploratory glance round the big

room. 'You came alone?'

'Yes, *signore*, I did!'

The light eyes swept over her in a swift and icy appraisal, bringing colour to her cheeks and the light of battle to her green eyes. She felt she had suffered quite enough indignity at this man's hands already, by being kept waiting, without being made to feel like some prize animal he was considering buying.

'You know my cousin, I believe.'

So Paolo Veronese was his cousin, and she had no doubt at all now that this was the formidable Alexei Romano, the big man himself. Not the crabby old man she had visualised, but a much more formidable prospect altogether.

She remembered, ruefully, her wish to have five minutes alone with the guardian of little Gino, but five minutes alone with this man would certainly not have the effect she had envisaged. He was very unlikely to be crushed by any condemnation of him as a bully, nor would he care tuppence for her opinion of him, good or bad.

'If you refer to Signor Veronese,' she said, striving to sound cool and aloof, 'we met yesterday.'

Her determination to remain cool and calm was rapidly losing ground to the strangely disturbing effect he was having on her senses. She could much more easily see now how he could command obedience and awe, not only from his staff and his family, but from strangers like her host as well. No wonder the secretary had been so shocked at her offhand agreement to see him.

'I was sitting on the quay yesterday when Signor Veronese and the little boy came along,' she informed him. 'And we passed the time of day.'

'Which was quite sufficient invitation for Paolo!' Again that cool, appraising glance swept over her. 'You are a very beautiful young woman.'

The words were without a hint of compliment or flattery, merely a statement of fact, and Storm resented them. It was obvious what he was implying about the meeting and it made her angry to be so misjudged.

'I believe I was the one who spoke first,' she told him, stiffly resentful. 'Not with any ulterior motive, but because the little boy was laughing, and it's an English custom to be polite and friendly.' She made the last statement pointedly, and again that faint tilt at one corner of his mouth betrayed a hint of amusement.

'But my cousin was only too willing to further the acquaintance, I have no doubt,' he said quietly, in his precise English. 'Do you intend seeing Paolo again, Miss Gavin?'

Storm felt anger and resentment churning away inside her, but a strange kind of excitement too, as if he presented a challenge that she would not be able to resist. He had absolutely no right to question her about her meeting with Paolo Veronese, whether he was his cousin or not, and she had no intention of letting him get away with it.

'That,' she told him firmly, 'surely depends

upon Signor Veronese and myself.'

'Not quite!' The quiet voice had an edge of steel that matched the glittering eyes. 'Paolo is not a complete fool!'

'You mean you'd——' Storm stared at him, her green eyes kindling dangerously. 'If your cousin chooses to let you—threaten him, *signore*, I suppose that's his affair, but I for one take exception to your attitude, and if that's all you have to say to me, I'll——'

'It is not,' he interrupted brusquely. 'I am simply seeking to establish that you are what you claimed to be when you spoke to my cousin, Miss Gavin, or if you are merely one of his—*fantòcci!*'

The tone of his voice was enough to convey all too clearly more or less what the word meant, and Storm clenched her hands tightly on the clasp of her handbag. She was trembling like a leaf and had never felt so angry and helpless in her life.

'I fail to see how it can possibly concern you,' she said in a small tight voice, 'but I'm a children's nurse, as I told Signor Veronese. And now, *signore*, I'm leaving. I refuse to stay here another minute and listen to your insults. You have absolutely no right to speak to me in this way, and I demand an apology!'

The air between them was taut as a drumskin, and the light blue eyes burned into her with a sensation like fire and ice, sending a shudder through her whole body. 'You came here this morning quite alone, *signorina*, and you apparently spoke first to my cousin yesterday, also when you were alone. I was entitled to assume what I did. An Italian girl would have been much more careful of her reputation.'

'I'm not an Italian girl!' Storm retorted swiftly. 'And in the circumstances I can only thank heaven for it! I still think you owe me an apology for what you've said to me!'

For a moment the icy scrutiny continued, then the tight mouth seemed to ease slightly and he inclined his head, very briefly, as if reluctantly acknowledging her right to an apology. 'Very well, *signorina*, it seems I have misjudged you, and I was perhaps too harsh. It would appear that your claim to be a children's nurse is true after all!'

'I can't imagine why you should have doubted it!' Storm told him. She felt horribly shaken by the events of the past few minutes, and wondered if anyone ever emerged unscathed from an encounter with this man.

He resented her temerity in answering him back, that was evident from his expression, and for a moment she wondered if he would simply turn and walk out of the room, but then, once again, the tension eased. 'I know my cousin, Miss Gavin,' he told her quietly. 'And you are obviously not only very attractive, but used to going around alone. It is a combination that Paolo would find irresistible.'

'You took me for a—a pick-up?' she suggested, wondering if the colloquialism was beyond him. She was quiet-voiced herself despite the turmoil of her thoughts.

Remembering Paolo Veronese's well-practised gallantry she was forced to admit that Alexei Romano's suspicions had probably been founded on experience, and she hastily lowered her eyes when she saw confirmation of it in his. 'It was a natural assumption, *signorina*.' He put a hand to the back of his head suddenly, brushing the thick dark hair absently as he stood in front of her, then with one hand he indicated that she should take one of the armchairs. After a brief hesitation she walked across and sat down again, sitting primly with her two feet on the floor and not crossing one leg over the other as she would more normally have done.

The pale green dress felt suddenly much flimsier than it really was, and she was inordinately conscious of the low fastening at the neckline, so that she put up a hand to it, her fingers surreptitiously pulling the two sides of the collar together.

He remained standing, and Storm guessed he intended keeping the upper hand. 'You were on the point of leaving when I came in?' he asked quietly.

He took a cigarette from a box on the table and lit it, the flame of the lighter throwing the hard, clean lines of his features into relief for a second, so that he looked more than ever like a bronze sculpture. Exhaling the smoke slowly from his nostrils gave him a curiously primitive look that was infinitely disturbing and sent an involuntary shiver along her spine.

He did not, she noticed, offer her a cigarette, and

she could well imagine that he was a man who disliked seeing women smoke and would therefore not even offer one out of politeness.

'I was leaving because I considered I'd waited quite long enough,' she told him, and one brow ascended swiftly while the light eyes narrowed behind the spiral of smoke from the cigarette.

'Even though you saw fit to be an hour late for your appointment?'

Storm felt herself flushing warmly again, and tilted her chin defiantly. 'I'm no more accustomed to being ordered to keep appointments that are none of my seeking than I am to being kept waiting, Signor Romano.' She looked at him steadily, her green eyes bright with defiance. 'I assume you *are* Signor Romano?' The name was niggling at her memory again, as she tried to remember where she had heard the name before.

He inclined his head, seemingly unimpressed by her effort to put him in his place. 'I do not usually have to identify myself, Miss Gavin. I am Alexei Romano.'

His self-confidence, she realised, was virtually unshakeable, but some small spark of determination made her affect a coolness she was far from feeling as he looked down at her with those ice-cool eyes. 'I've been trying to think where I've heard the name before, Signor Romano,' she told him in a light, slightly breathless voice.

For a moment he said nothing, but regarded her steadily through the haze of blue smoke, feet slightly apart, his dark, Slavonic-looking features in shadow. A tall and rather menacing figure who looked as if he could have crushed her in one hand.

'So,' he said at last, 'you did not know my name, and yet you came here to see me, and alone.'

'The fact that I came had nothing to do with you,' Storm protested hurriedly, perhaps too hurriedly. 'It was because you were the little boy's guardian. He looked so—so sad that I was—touched.'

'And you wished to see for yourself the brute who was ill-treating him and making him look so sad, yes?' There was an icy glitter in his eyes again, and she felt sure he resented being accused of ill-treating the little boy more than he had anything else so far.

'I didn't say that,' she objected mildly; too mildly, it seemed, for it was obvious he did not believe her.

It came to her then why the name had been familiar when she had heard her host mention it. Last year some time, in a British newspaper, she remembered reading something about a millionaire industrialist being killed in a car crash and a tiny boy being left heir to a vast fortune. The man's name had been Romano, she felt sure, but this little boy was called Targhese, according to Paolo Veronese.

'Gino is my late brother's child, Miss Gavin.' Alexei Romano's voice recalled her, and she looked up hastily at the dark shadowed face with its light eyes. 'I am his guardian, since his mother is also dead, and I do as well as I can for him.'

'Oh, I'm sure you do, Signor Romano!'

She was very sure of it, suddenly. No matter what her opinion of him was in regard to herself and the way he seemed to rule everyone else with a rod of iron, she really felt that his affection for the little boy, Gino, was genuine. That difference in name could probably be accounted for by circumstances that a man like Alexei Romano would not dream of mentioning.

'Is there something wrong, Miss Gavin?'

His voice was edged with impatience and Storm dragged herself back from the realms of speculation, looking up to find him regarding her steadily, almost as if he followed her thoughts. He said nothing about it, however, but ran the fingers of one hand through the thick hair that covered half his forehead, and surprised her with a small, very brief smile that softened the sculptured lines of his face for only a second.

'You will find, Miss Gavin, that that large-eyed, soulful look is deceptive. Gino *does* miss his father, I cannot deny it, but twenty years ago if you had met my cousin Paolo, you would have seen a child very much like Gino is now.'

'Oh, I see!'

She found it easy to accept the fact, but, while she was as concerned with Gino's welfare, as with all children's, she began to wonder when Alexei Romano was going to bring the conversation round to matters more pertinent to her visit. It startled her to discover that she was finding him so fascinating as a man that she was reluctant to have things brought to a head, and perhaps never have the opportunity of speaking to him again.

'But he still touches your heart, yes?' He asked the question softly, and Storm brought herself back to earth, raising reproachful eyes to him.

'Well, it *was* his parents that were killed in that car crash,' she told him. 'And no amount of wealth is going to compensate for that.'

Alexei Romano narrowed his eyes, nodding his head slowly. 'So—you *did* know who I was!'

'I'd heard of you before,' she allowed. 'But I just couldn't think why the name was familiar—now I've remembered.'

'Thank you!'

There was sarcasm in the deep, quiet voice and she thought she detected a glimpse of ironic amusement in his eyes for a moment, but she guessed his pride had taken a blow, however small, from her admission.

'Oh, my host mentioned your business interests,' she explained carefully. 'But I was trying to remember about the car crash—I knew it was something about a child. That's all that interested me. Millionaire industrialists are of little interest to me, Signor Romano.'

He stood silent and contemplative for a moment while Storm sat and waited, surprising herself with her willingness to do so. 'Your being a children's nurse is the reason I sent for you.' Storm looked at him in disbelief, her heart doing a sudden and quite alarming tattoo against her ribs when she realised the implication of the statement.

'It—it is?'

'Paolo tells me that you are seeking employment as a children's nurse.'

Storm nodded, eyes hazy, her lips parted slightly as she gazed at him. 'Yes, yes, I am, but——'

A long hand waved aside explanations. 'You are fully qualified to cater for the needs of a small child?'

'Yes, I am.'

She could scarcely believe that she was hearing him aright. That he was actually suggesting that she should come and work for him, taking care of the little boy he set such store by. Once he had satisfied himself that she was not simply one of Paolo Veronese's more casual acquaintances, of course, and she could not blame him for that.

It was difficult to believe that she was not imagining the whole thing, that it was not real at all. But there was nothing unreal about Alexei Romano as he stood there in front of her. He was very much flesh and blood and very disturbingly masculine.

'But, Signor Romano,' she ventured, bringing herself back to earth, 'if it's for Gino, surely he needs to go to school, not have the services of a nurse.'

Those icy eyes were regarding her again with dis-

34

approval, making it evident that he did not like having his decisions questioned. 'Gino is not yet five years old,' he told her. 'And *I* will judge when he is ready for school, *signorina*.'

'Yes, yes, of course.' It was not an ideal situation, with the little boy so near school age, but it would suit her well enough for the time being.

'I need someone to care for him until he is of school age, but there is no harm in him receiving some basic instruction in certain subjects.'

'Basic instruction in——'

The expression on the dark, chiselled features cut her short. 'Please allow me to finish, Miss Gavin.' The autocratically assured air put her firmly in her place again, and he expelled a long plume of smoke from between tight lips before he spoke again. 'Gino, so my cousin tells me, appeared to like you during your brief meeting, and since you are looking for employment as a children's nurse, I think you will prove useful.'

He leaned over and ground out the remains of the cigarette in an ashtray on the table beside her, long brown fingers crushing down relentlessly. The table was low and the movement brought him intimately close for the brief time it took the smouldering stub to die. As he drew back the back of his hand brushed lightly against her knee; the warm, almost sensual touch of it startled her so much that she instinctively drew back from it, fighting against the ever-increasing excitement that welled up inside her.

This man was a stranger, a wealthy, remote stranger who had offered her a job, nothing more, and it was ridiculous for her to be so affected by him. It was, nevertheless, very difficult to remain unconscious of him as a man when he stood so close, his hands behind his back, like some tall, dark Nemesis looming over her.

'I must ask you for an immediate answer,' he told her. 'In the event of you refusing the post, I shall have to make other arrangements.'

It was quite evident that he considered the likelihood of a refusal most improbable, and was possibly ready to conclude the interview there and then. Storm's head was spinning with a thousand and one reasons why she should not take the job he offered, not least the fact that she was not a qualified teacher and he had said he wanted some tuition for the boy, however basic.

Heaven knew what academic qualifications he imagined she possessed, but obviously something more than she had. He might even be under the impression that she spoke Italian. There was the prospect of having him as her employer too. He was arrogant, confident to the point of being overbearing and quite the most disturbing man she had ever met, and she must be quite crazy to even consider working for him, but the truth was she *did* want to.

After a long silence, during which time she felt those disturbing eyes watching her closely, she looked up and took a deep breath. Before she could say what she had to say, however, that cool, slightly impatient voice cut across her thoughts.

'I assume that you are attempting to make up your mind, Miss Gavin,' he said. 'I must remind you that I asked for an immediate answer.'

'I was about to——' she began, but was again cut short by that impatient voice.

'It is surely not such a difficult decision to make!'

'But I'm not a schoolteacher, Signor Romano!' She was determined to be heard this time. 'I'm not qualified to teach, even young children, like Gino. I'm a nurse, a nanny, if you like, but not a teacher.'

Another impatient frown and she saw the likelihood of her getting the job slipping away if she raised any more obstacles. Alexei Romano was obviously not a patient man and what little patience he possessed was rapidly running out.

'You may call yourself what you wish,' he informed her brusquely. 'I am only concerned with your ability to care for Gino. If you are not capable of doing that then I shall conclude that you have been deceiving me after all, Miss Gavin.'

There was a chilling threat in the cool voice, and Storm looked up at him indignantly; her professional ability in question was something she would not stand for. 'I've done nothing of the sort!' she denied.

'Then I take it you accept my offer. At five years old Gino does not need a university professor!'

She was breathless and a little bewildered from

being swept along at such a breakneck pace, bent and manoeuvred to suit this man's purpose, and she could only look at him, wide-eyed, for several moments and shake her head slowly.

'I—I could try,' she said. 'The little I've seen of Gino, I like him.'

'It is more important that Gino likes *you*,' Alexei Romano informed her shortly. 'That is the reason I am employing you. Gino has met you, at least briefly, and you will not be completely strange to him.'

Storm yielded gracefully; there was little else she could do, she felt. It would be fighting a losing battle to try and do anything else, for it was obvious that once Alexei Romano had decided on something, it had to be.

'I'll do my best,' she promised, and he nodded, evidently considering the matter settled. 'But, Signor Romano, I——' Another impatient frown condemned her persistence. 'I—I don't know if you realise it, but I don't speak any Italian.'

'Of course you do not, otherwise you would have used it, however badly.' The cool eyes glittered briefly with derisive amusement. 'Most people with a smattering of a foreign tongue insist on using it, no matter how unintelligible it may be to the natives.'

Storm ignored the apparent slur on lesser mortals, and pressed home her point. 'As long as you understand that anything I teach Gino will have to be in English.'

'Of course. I wish him to speak English as fluently as he does Italian. You will suit admirably for a short time.'

'Until he starts school?'

'And probably for a time after that,' he informed her. 'Until he settles down to the routine of school. It would distress him if he was suddenly deprived of someone he had become attached to.'

Like a favourite teddy bear, Storm thought a little hysterically, and wondered how on earth she had got herself involved like this. She had merely passed the time of day with an attractive man and a small boy who happened to be passing, and here she was, only a day later, faced with the prospect of staying in Italy for an indefinite period, in charge of a child who was worth a fortune.

Her friends in England would not believe it, she scarcely believed it herself yet. 'I—I hope I can come up to your expectations, *signore*,' she said.

The ice-blue eyes regarded her steadily. 'I hope so too, Miss Gavin. You will start tomorrow morning and you will, of course, be paid your salary for the whole month. My secretary will go into the details with you; if you have any queries, please see him.'

He seemed prepared to leave it there and half turned towards the door. 'Oh, but, Signor Romano——!' He looked down at her impatiently, and Storm had the feeling that only with difficulty did he refrain from telling her to forget the whole thing. But Gino liked her, and she suited his purpose at the moment.

His eyes were narrowed again and the sculptured bronze features had a hard, ruthless look that made her pulses flutter nervously as she hastily avoided his eyes. 'Do you wish to work for me or not, Miss Gavin?' he asked and, almost without realising it, Storm nodded. 'Then you will do as I decide, *when* I decide. Good morning, Miss Gavin!'

He turned on his heel and strode across the room, his long muscular legs covering the distance in seconds, while Storm sat there staring after him. Then, as he bent to retrieve the riding crop he had thrown down on his way in, she got to her feet, her mouth set determinedly.

'Signor Romano!'

He turned swiftly, ice-blue eyes glittering warningly, the crop tapping against one shiny boot. '*Signorina?*'

She hesitated to make the objection in the face of such obvious discouragement, and shook her head rather vaguely. 'I—you didn't bother to ask if it was convenient for me to start tomorrow morning,' she told him, much more mildly than she had intended, and she saw his lips tighten ominously.

The fascinating face with its high, Slavonic-looking cheekbones betrayed the beginnings of a formidable temper, and the crop, gripped hard in strong fingers, tapped threateningly against a polished leather boot as he stared at her.

'You told me that you were at present unemployed, Miss Gavin, and seeking another post. I have offered you employment, but if you wish to work for me there is one thing you should get clear from the beginning. I expect to have my wishes carried out without question and without delay. Do you understand?'

Her own temper was threatening to show itself and ruin the whole thing, so she swallowed hard on the word that rose to her lips, and instead nodded slowly. 'Yes, Signor Romano.'

'Good!'

He turned on his heel again and was gone, the double doors closing firmly behind him, while Storm subsided breathlessly into a chair, shaking her head in disbelief, both at her own compliance and at the events of the past few minutes.

She supposed she should feel honoured to have been chosen for the job, and certainly staying on in Bellabaia would mean she could see more of Paolo Veronese, her employer permitting, of course. But of one thing she was quite certain. She was going to find it an uphill fight keeping her temper with an employer as insufferably arrogant as Alexei Romano.

CHAPTER THREE

STORM found herself dismayingly nervous when she came to report to the Villa Romano next morning. It was partly, she realised as she walked down the shady approach to the villa, because she feared Alexei Romano would have had second thoughts since yesterday and she would perhaps be summarily sent packing even before she had set foot in the place again.

She was admitted, however, by the same solemn-faced manservant she had seen yesterday, but this time he asked her to wait in the hall while he fetched Signor Romano's secretary, the young man she had spoken to on the telephone. When he came soft-footed from the stairs behind her, he bowed over her hand and introduced himself as Rafael Caldorini.

He was very good-looking, something she had half expected, and he too reminded her of those voluptuous young men pictured on the frescoed wall behind him, a comparison borne out by the gleam of pleasure in his dark eyes when he bowed over her hand. He was much less tall than either his employer or Paolo Veronese, and he had curly black hair and a smooth olive brown skin. He would, Storm thought, become very plump in a few years from now.

'I am to tell you of the financial arrangements made by Signor Romano, *signorina*,' he informed her softly, and Storm nodded, relieved that it was him and not his employer she was to see this morning.

'Yes, of course, Signor Caldorini.'

Her smile seemed to encourage him and the dark eyes glowed warmly. 'You will come with me, *per favore, signorina*?'

'Signorina Gavin!' The wide hall echoed to Paolo Veronese's deep, warm voice and Storm turned, smiling at him rather cautiously. Now that she was to work for his cousin, she was a little uncertain just how she should behave towards him. She need have had no such doubts, however, for he seemed to have the situation well in hand. 'You are to work for us! Mmm!' He kissed the tips of his fingers extravagantly. 'Oh, I am so—*molto felice*!'

'Thank you, *signore*.'

She was very conscious of a knowing and slightly resentful gleam in the secretary's eyes as he watched them, and wished, at the moment anyway, that Paolo Veronese would be less Latin in his enthusiasm. It had been he, of course, who was responsible for her having the job, but she needed no second guess at what had prompted the generous gesture. It showed clearly enough in the warm dark eyes that looked down at her so meaningly.

'I must show you our gardens,' he told her, and Storm saw the frown that marred Rafael Caldorini's good looks, forestalling her own objection.

'But, *signore*,' he interposed softly, 'I was told——'

'I will bring the *signorina* to the study when we are ready, Rafael,' Paolo Veronese informed him loftily. 'You need not wait.'

'*Si, signore*.' A slight bob of the black head acknowledged defeat, and the secretary disappeared back up the stairs to the shadowed gallery behind them.

Paolo smiled down at her, well pleased with his minor triumph, but Storm was less happy about the secretary's dismissal. There was the question of what Alexei Romano would have to say about her disobeying his instructions on her very first day, and she was not happy about it.

'You do not mind that I sent him away, *signorina*?'

His confident smile dismissed the very idea of her objecting, and she was unable to resist a smile at the bold, persuasive charm of him. He was almost as self-confident as his cousin but much less aggressive and arrogant.

She shook her head, pushing back the tawny hair from her forehead with one hand. 'I'm flattered, Signor Veronese, but I really should have gone with Signor Caldorini. Signor Romano will probably be very angry with me for not doing as he instructed, and on my very first day here.'

Paolo Veronese made a rueful face, his hands spread in resignation. 'I suppose you are right,' he admitted. 'But first, *signorina*——' He took her

44

two hands in his own and lifted them to his lips, his mouth warmly pressed to her fingers. 'First you will agree to call me Paolo, yes?'

'I—I don't know.' She felt an insistent tap-tapping at her ribs where her heart responded to that very Latin gesture, and the brown fingers that squeezed hers gently. 'I'm not sure that Signor Romano would approve.'

'Ah, *assùrdo*! Why should Alexei mind if you call me by my name?'

Storm could think of no good reason why he should object, but she had no doubt that he would, because he would not like her being on too familiar terms with his cousin. 'I don't really know,' she confessed.

'Then you will call me Paolo, yes?'

The dark gaze and the deep, persuasive voice were irresistible, and she laughed softly, unconsciously provocative. 'All right, I'll call you Paolo!'

'*Bene! Bellissima!*' He kissed her fingers again fervently. 'Now—we go and see the gardens, no?'

'I don't think so,' Storm told him, and could not resist a smile for the genuine disappointment in his eyes. 'I'm sure there's a lot to see, and——'

'And I shall show it to you, hmm? Not just the garden, but everything! The countryside, Naples —ah, *bellissima Napoli*!' He kissed the tips of his fingers again, his dark eyes beaming at her persuasively so that she was bound to respond.

'I'd love to see everything there is to see,' she said, 'and I'd like you to show me, Paolo, but I'm

45

not sure yet how much time I'll have.'

For a moment he simply looked at her in silence, then he leaned forward suddenly and kissed her lightly but firmly on her mouth, startling her into a soft cry of surprise. 'Storm, *cara mia*, you worry too much about Alexei, I think. I did not get you this post so that you could spend every minute of the day and night with Gino. *Comprende?*' He swept his gaze over her face and figure and smiled. 'You are much too beautiful, *cara*, to waste on a *bambino*!'

Such words had a heady effect, even though she knew quite well their meaning was only superficial, and she could feel the rapid warning thud of her heart as she sought to remain sensible, and not be swept along by something that was wellnigh irresistible.

'But I do *work* for Signor Romano,' she reminded him, and he shrugged with Latin carelessness.

'Even Alexei does not expect you to spend every minute with Gino. He will not—how is it?—eat you if you spend some time with me. In fact he will expect it in the circumstances.'

In the circumstances! He had inveigled his cousin into employing her to look after the boy, but, as he said, even Alexei Romano would not be in ignorance of the real reason behind the recommendation, and she wondered suddenly if it had happened before.

'Does—does your cousin often take people on

46

your recommendation?' she asked, and he looked at her steadily for a moment before answering, then he gently stroked her cheek with one caressing finger.

'No, *cara mia*, Alexei has never before approved of my taste. You are to be congratulated!' He smiled, the gentle finger moving hypnotically against her cheek. 'As for the rest of the family, they will adore you.'

'The—the rest of the family?' She looked startled, all sorts of new possibilities arising. 'How many more of you are there, Paolo?'

'Only two.' He shrugged carelessly. 'You cannot count Rafael, although he lives here.' He raised her fingers to his lips again. 'Do not be timid, *graziosa mia*, no one will trouble you. There is only Lisetta and my mama that you have not met.'

She did not ask who Lisetta was, but assumed she would be either an aunt or a sister, living in the family home, for she knew it was quite common for Italian families to live all under one roof. 'Oh well,' she sighed resignedly, 'I expect I'll get used to you all.'

'*Si*, of course you will!' He caught her unawares again and kissed her mouth. 'Now, if you will not see the gardens with me, we will go and find Rafael before he has time to tell Alexei about me!' It was quite obvious, she thought, that there was quite a bit of competition between Paolo and his cousin's good-looking secretary.

He took her hand and drew her with him across

the hall to that rather awe-inspiring marble stair-case, taking the wide steps with long familiar strides so that she was hard put to keep up with him.

The floor up here was carpeted, with thick luxurious pile into which she sank, ankle deep, and she had barely a chance to notice more than the fact that the walls were white-painted and hung with portraits, before a door opened further along the gallery and Rafael Caldorini appeared.

He looked at Paolo with what Storm recognised as a malicious gleam in his dark eyes, and he bobbed his head briefly. 'Signor Romano asks that you go to him *immediatamente, signore.*'

'*Si, si, ben intéso!*' Paolo frowned and sighed as he raised Storm's hand to his lips, kissing her fingers lightly. 'I will see you again soon, *cara mia. Arrivederci!*'

'*Signorina!*' Rafael Caldorini's soft voice recalled her as she watched Paolo hurry along the gallery, and she smiled at him apologetically.

'I'm sorry, Signor Caldorini. I hope you didn't have too much difficulty explaining to Signor Romano—I mean about my not coming with you the first time.'

'Ah no, *signorina.*' Eloquent shoulders accepted the inevitable. 'Signor Romano understands.' For a moment the bold black eyes met hers and she felt the colour in her cheeks at the unmistakable implication she saw there. It was obvious that, at least as far as some of the Romano household was concerned, she was another of Paolo's affairs and quite casually accepted as such.

He led her along the gallery to a room that obviously did service as a study—a long, cool room, less ornate that the room she had seen downstairs yesterday, white-walled and dazzlingly bright with the sun that came in through the high arched windows.

A flickering little pattern of lights played over the high carved ceiling, and it took her a moment or two to recognise it for what it was. The fluttering, ever-changing pattern was reflected off water. Possibly a pool or a fountain, for it was much too high up for the reflection to be from the sea, and there was a garden below the window, because she could detect the unmistakable sweet and slightly heady scent of lemons.

Rafael Caldorini seated himself behind a desk in the centre of the room and indicated that she should take the chair facing him, then he shuffled for a moment or two through some papers—a gesture meant to impress her, she felt.

'Ah! Now, *signorina*!' He beamed at her across the desk, and began to explain the financial arrangements that his employer had made for her. They were generous in the extreme and she had no complaints, but he did not once ask if they suited her, or whether she had had second thoughts about taking the post. Such a thing was not to be considered, she guessed. No one would ever refuse to work for the Romanos.

Having disposed of the arrangements to his satisfaction, he got to his feet again, bowing briefly, a wide smile on his face as if he was rather pleased with his own efforts. 'I shall now take you to see Gino,' he informed her. 'He is waiting for you, *signorina.*'

Apparently she was to be plunged headlong into her work without delay, but Storm was not prepared to be rushed along at the pace that seemed to be taken for normal in the Romano household. Whoever it was that said the Latin races preferred the principle of *mañana* had obviously never had contact with Alexei Romano and his staff.

She had been a little dubious about living in the same house as Paolo Veronese, for obvious reasons, and wondered if it would be possible for her to come daily to the villa instead of living in. 'I wonder, Signor Caldorini,' she said, as she followed him across the room, 'if it would be possible for me to stay on at the Villa Lucia for the time being.'

He turned swiftly, his dark eyes regarding her for a moment in puzzled silence. 'You do not wish to work for Signor Romano, after all, *signorina*?' he asked, and Storm smiled, shaking her head at his misunderstanding.

'Oh no, not that at all,' she denied. 'But I thought perhaps, for the time being, until I get more used to—to everything, I could go on staying where I am and come along here each day.'

Dark brows drew together in a frown of deep concentration. 'I cannot answer that, *signorina*, but if you wish me to, I will speak of the matter to Signor Romano.'

Storm was doubtful that any suggestion coming from her stood very much chance of being adopted, but she smiled her gratitude for his offer. 'I'd be very grateful if you'd mention it,' she told him. 'I'm really quite happy where I am.'

Incredibly, she realised that the dark eyes were speculating on the extent of her gratitude, but before she had time to do more than register the fact that Rafael Caldorini was another good reason for not staying there, he was bobbing his head briefly and politely.

'*Molto bene, signorina,*' he said softly.

He held open the door for her, indicating another, immediately across the gallery, and leaned over to knock on it lightly. Without waiting for an invitation he opened it and signed to Storm to go in first.

The sun was as bright as it had been in the study, but a striped awning shaded out the worst of the dazzle and extended out over a small balcony beyond an open french window. Out there she could see Gino, the little boy, sitting curled up on a white-painted reclining chair piled high with striped cushions. He looked lonely and rather bored.

He looked up when the door opened and a second later came running across the room, his small thin face curious but smiling. His huge dark eyes looked from her to Rafael Caldorini.

'*Signorina.*' He bobbed his head politely. 'Welcome to Villa Romano!'

Storm smiled down at him, her heart touched again by that oddly pathetic little face and the grave, grown-up welcome. No matter what his uncle said about it, she still believed that it was because he was unhappy that he looked the way he did, and she found it difficult to believe that Paolo Veronese had ever looked quite so heartrendingly soulful.

'Hello, Gino,' she said. 'Didn't your uncle tell you that I was coming to look after you?'

'Ah, *si, si, eccètto*——' He shrugged off whatever it was that concerned him, and took one of her hands, pulling her across the room and out on to the balcony to where he had been sitting. 'Signorina Gavin, *desidero andare*——'

Storm placed a gentle finger over his mouth. 'You have to speak English, Gino,' she told him. 'I don't speak Italian.'

Once more the black head bobbed, gravely polite. 'I am sorry, *signorina*.'

Storm turned and saw the secretary still standing just inside the room, watching them, and she smiled. 'Thank you, Signor Caldorini. You won't forget to mention that matter to Signor Romano, will you?'

'*Certamente, signorina!*'

She smiled again and immediately reminded herself that she must not be too encouraging, when she saw the quick, dark glow in the man's eyes. 'Thank you.'

The black head bobbed in the customary brief bow and white teeth showed briefly in a wide smile across the olive-skinned face. '*Grazie, signorina.*'

Gino offered her his seat with a flourish she felt would have been worthy of Paolo Veronese at his most gallant, and she accepted it with a slight inclination of her head, looking down at the garden below the balcony.

It was terraced to fit into the steepness of the cliff side, but it flourished on that dark fertile soil as the farmers' crops did. There were shading trees around a pool with white stone seats surrounding it, the water making the same shifting light patterns on this ceiling as they had in the study.

Geraniums and roses spilled in profusion everywhere, crowding the steps and the edge of the pool. Dark, plume-topped cypresses looking almost black in contrast to the bright sun and myriad colours around them. There were even one or two white marble figures, slender, rounded goddesses with heads bowed coyly, half hidden behind the yellow, fluffy boughs of mimosa.

The whole thing stood above the blue Mediterranean like a floating paradise, and Storm thought she had never seen anything quite so beautiful in her life. It was cool and lovely and very inviting on such a hot day.

'Signorina Gavin!' Gino was tugging at her arm, reminding her that he was there, and she turned back to him with a smile. 'You are going to stay?' he asked.

Storm put down her handbag beside the seat, and put an arm round his thin little body, drawing him close. 'I hope so, Gino,' she said. 'If we get along together.'

'And we will have—fun, no?'

'I hope so,' Storm agreed, wondering just how much he was in the picture, and how much she was expected to tell him about his uncle's plans. 'But we must work too.'

He half leaned against her, looking up with those huge, persuasive dark eyes, then he smiled. 'We will go sailing, *si, signorina?*' he said softly. 'I have friend with a fishing boat and he say he will take me sailing one day.'

It seemed a pity to have to disappoint him so soon, but she doubted if Alexei Romano would approve of his nephew going sailing in one of the fishing boats, and it seemed pretty obvious too that he expected her to amuse him rather than teach him.

'Perhaps,' she allowed vaguely. 'But for the moment there are other things to think about, Gino. Can you count, for instance?'

It was evident that this was the first obstacle, and Storm recognised it with a brief sigh. There was a definite suggestion of a sulk about that full lower lip and, sad little boy or not, she began to suspect that Gino had quite a lot in common with his autocratic uncle. He disliked not having things his own way.

'Why do I have to learn to count?' he demanded, and Storm smiled.

54

'Because everyone has to,' she explained patiently. 'You want to grow up and be able to run the business like your uncle does, don't you?'

Gino shrugged, rebellion in his eyes. 'I would rather go sailing,' he insisted firmly.

'I'm sure you would.' She was tempted by the appeal of those huge eyes, but knew she had to be firm if they were to make any progress at all. 'But we have work to do, Gino.'

'And if I do not *wish* to work?' There was speculation and a look of challenge in his eyes that reminded her again of his uncle. There was altogether too much of Alexei Romano's implacable will in this seemingly frail little boy, which probably meant that he took after his father, and she sighed inwardly at the prospect before her.

'If you do that, your uncle will send me away,' she told him quietly, and Gino considered that for a moment.

'*Si, molto bene,*' he agreed gravely at last. 'I work.'

She had no time to express approval of the decision, before the door opened, and Gino was off in a moment, flying across the room in a flurry of arms and legs.

'Zio Alexei, Zio Alexei!' he cried as he flung himself at his uncle, and Storm got to her feet, annoyed to find herself feeling quite ridiculously nervous and wondering why Alexei Romano should have such an effect on her.

He was not dressed for riding this morning, but

wearing a light grey suit and a white shirt that served to emphasise the dark bronze colour of his skin, but that irresistible magnetism she had experienced yesterday struck her again like a blow when he walked across the room.

'*Calmo, piccolo!*' One large hand ruffled the boy's hair and he spoke softly, gently in Italian. 'Miss Gavin.'

He stood in front of her, his hand still on the boy's head, his feet slightly apart, a stance that somehow made him look even more overpowering. The slim-fitting trousers emphasized lean hips and strong muscular legs and the jacket swung open showing a shirt of fine white silk, like the one he had worn yesterday, and which again showed the shadowy darkness of his body through its fine texture.

There was more speculation than coldness in the light eyes at the moment, although she thought he was here in response to her request to Rafael Caldorini. He made no secret of his inspection of her pale green sleeveless dress and the lacy white shoes that complemented it and once again she was made conscious of the fairly low neckline and put up a hand in a gesture that was almost defensive.

He looked at her steadily until her heart was rapping at her ribs as she waited for whatever he had to say. 'You wish to alter the arrangements I have made, so I understand,' he said.

'No, not exactly,' Storm denied, shaking her head. 'Actually we made no arrangements about

56

where I should stay, *signore*. At least nothing was said to me about them.'

'You dislike your room here?'

She shook her head. 'I haven't seen my room, Signor Romano.'

The way those dark brows drew together boded ill for Rafael Caldorini, she suspected, and wondered if she had been a little unfair to him.

'Then you have not brought your luggage with you?' She shook her head. 'I will send someone for it, *signorina*.'

'But—I thought it might be possible for me to stay on at the Villa Lucia for a while,' she ventured.

'You are perhaps fearful for your reputation?' The question was put in a soft voice, steel-edged, so that she was left in no doubt of his opinion, or what the outcome of the request would be.

'No,' she denied, and would have said more, but was given no chance.

'You need not be concerned,' he told her. 'There are two other ladies in the house as well as the servants.'

'I know, but——'

'If it is not the moral aspect that troubles you,' again he interrupted her, 'then why do you wish to change the arrangements I have made? You are accustomed to living in the house of your employer, are you not?'

'Yes, yes, of course I am.' She was annoyed to find herself so pliable, so unwilling to insist on her own opinions. 'I didn't intend making a major issue of this, Signor Romano, I just thought——'

'Whatever you thought, Miss Gavin, it is out of the question.' He pushed one hand into a trousers pocket, relaxed and yet fully confident that he was in full command of the situation. 'I am employing you to take care of Gino at all times—day and night.'

'Oh, but surely,' Storm protested, 'I get *some* time for myself!'

'Naturally,' he agreed calmly. 'Once Gino is in bed for the night, there will be little call upon your services and you may then do more or less as you please. But you will never stay away from the villa all night, no matter what your reason, is that quite clear?'

Somehow he made her possible reasons for staying away at night sound far from the innocent one behind her request and she looked at him challengingly from beneath her long lashes. 'I don't like what you're implying, *signore*,' she told him. 'I had no intention of living *here* and staying out all night, and I resent the suggestion that I would.'

The ice-blue eyes surveyed her coolly for a moment and she found her own gaze lingering on that strong, firm jaw and the deep cleft in the square chin. She found Alexei Romano fascinating to a degree that disturbed her intensely. 'I assume you will be spending quite a lot of time with my cousin when you are not with Gino,' he said quietly. 'I have no doubt about his powers of persuasion, Miss Gavin. I am therefore insisting that you move into the Villa Romano and that you return here at a reasonable hour every night.'

'Where you can keep an eye on me!'

The angry retort was almost involuntary, but she was fighting a chaos of emotions and hardly knew what to think. She was angry, partly because she objected to being treated in such cavalier fashion, but also because she knew she would comply with his demands, sooner or later.

He held her angry gaze for a second in silence, then raised a brow in acknowledgement. 'Exactly!'

Her resentment showed plainly in her eyes as she faced him, her hands trembling so that she clenched them tight at her sides. 'I dislike having my way of life dictated to me, Signor Romano,' she told him, her voice shaking. 'I understood that slavery had been abolished, but judging by your behaviour, you seem to be living in the Middle Ages still, thinking you have the *droit du seigneur* over your employees!'

She felt a sudden shiver of panic as he stood there towering over her, and the look of savagery she had glimpsed on their first meeting was nothing to the expression that now showed taut and fierce on the hard, sculptured features. The ice-blue eyes were narrowed above those high cheekbones, and hard as blue steel.

'You will apologise, *signorina!*' His voice too, was as cold as ice, but still did not rise above its normal quiet pitch and she marvelled at his self-control. She would have refused, angrily, but something about this man filled her with emotions she had never experienced before, so that she was no longer sure of her own strength of will, and she stayed silent. 'Very well!' His mouth was a tight straight line. 'It is your own choice, Miss Gavin.'

For one panicky moment she wondered if he was going to strike her, but then Gino chose to intervene. His small, thin face looked puzzled and more soulful than ever as he looked up at his uncle and tugged at the sleeve of his jacket.

'Zio Alexei, *che c'è?*' he asked, but the icy gaze did not shift from Storm.

'*Stia calmo,* Gino,' he told the boy quietly.

Gino, however, was not prepared to keep quiet, he was curious as well as a little apprehensive, and he was enough of his uncle's nephew to want to know what was going on. He tugged at the jacket sleeve again, raising his voice.

'*Zio, che cosa è successo?*' he demanded.

The man's stern features softened for a moment and he looked down at him. '*Niente affato, piccolo,*' he said softly, and put a consoling hand on his head. '*Stia calmo, per favore.*'

'*Signorina?*'

Gino looked at her, frowning. He had probably never seen anyone defy his formidable uncle before, and he knew well enough which one of them was going to have to back down. He was merely reminding her, trying to have the episode over and done with.

Storm still hesitated. She did not want to leave and admit defeat so soon, but she was not sure that she was ready to eat humble pie either, and she must do one or the other now. Alexei Romano was looking at her again, waiting, and she felt a shiver along her spine again.

'*Signorina?*'

He echoed Gino's one-word question and it left the decision squarely with her. Without quite knowing what to do or say next, she stood there without moving, sensitive to every breath he took, and amazed at her own reaction to him as a man.

It seemed quite incredible that she should even consider backing down, but she knew she was bound to and she took a deep breath. 'I'm—I'm sorry, Signor Romano.'

'*Bene!*' he breathed softly, and she could have sworn that a glint of relief showed briefly in his eyes.

As for Gino, he obviously approved of the outcome and for a moment Storm felt like laughing hysterically at the whole unbelievable episode. She would never have acted with such compliance last year this time, in fact she would have immediately walked out and never come back. Her independence had always been dear to her, and yet here she was ready to swallow her pride so that she could remain in the employ of a man who behaved as if he had the power of life and death over her.

For a moment, as he leaned across to ruffle the boy's hair, his hand came in contact with her bare arm and she felt her pulses leap in response to his touch, drawing back instinctively. He looked at her steadily, closer now, and with a curious expression in his eyes. 'I beg your pardon, *signorina*,' he said softly.

Storm said nothing, but strove to steady her heart beat as it thudded wildly at her ribs. There was so much more than his arrogance that she was going to have to cope with, if she stayed on at the Villa Romano and she wondered if she had not perhaps bitten off more than she could chew.

CHAPTER FOUR

IT was something of a relief to Storm to learn that both the ladies of the Romano household were absent for the day, and she would not have to meet them, at least for a while. Signora Veronese, Paolo's mother, was away visiting her married daughter, and the mysterious Lisetta had an appointment with her dressmaker in Naples that apparently necessitated an all-day absence.

As both Paolo and Alexei Romano spent the rest of the day at the works in Naples Storm lunched alone with Gino in their makeshift schoolroom overlooking the garden. Dinner with Paolo, Gino and her employer proved more of an ordeal in the grand surroundings of the villa's dining-room, but she was thankful that at least she was spared the addition of two ladies who would probably disapprove of her being there at all.

If they were as close-knit a family as Paolo claimed they were, the women of the family might well resent the advent of a stranger in their midst, especially if she was a foreigner and taking charge of a child they were fond of.

Rafael Caldorini had informed her that she would be living as part of the family, since Gino had never been relegated to a nursery, so there was nothing she could do about sharing her meals only with him, but feeling as she did at the moment she felt she would have been more at home in the company of the domestic staff.

Her luggage was brought from the Villa Lucia during the morning and put in her room, as Alexei Romano had promised, and she supposed she should have been perfectly happy, but the thought of living *en famille* in a household that included Alexei Romano was surely daunting enough for anybody.

Thankfully she retired to her own room as soon as she had put Gino to bed, much to Paolo's disappointment, for he had had plans for them to spend the evening in Naples, dancing. She felt she simply had to have time to draw breath, some time to herself, and Paolo was not the most placid of companions.

She could find no fault with the room she had been given, indeed she was delighted with it. Like every other room she had seen so far, it was luxurious. Light and pretty and surprisingly feminine, so that she wondered who its last occupant had been.

The high ceiling was richly ornamented with scrolls and gilt curlicues and made her feel, yet again, as if she had stepped back several hundred years in time. A high wide window opened above the garden and the pool. Soft rugs, deep-piled carpet and, unbelievably, a lace-draped bed, all seemed to her to be slightly unreal, and she lay there in the morning cool, the following day, wondering how it all came to happen.

Who would have believed that three weeks ago when she left Mrs. Marley's in Surrey, she would so soon be living in a villa in Italy, *and* getting very generously paid for it? It was still a bit difficult for her to believe it all, and she only hoped she would not suddenly wake up and find it all a dream.

The thought clouding her waking peace this morning was the idea of meeting the two women of the household. It would be too optimistic to hope that neither of them would be a female version of Alexei Romano, and Storm pulled a face in sympathy with herself as she got out of bed.

Gino declared himself not yet ready to get up when she looked in on him, and she decided that it could do no harm to leave him where he was for a while, for he had already informed her that he never ate anything in the mornings. For herself, she was more than ready for rolls and coffee and she went downstairs in search of sustenance.

The kitchens, she knew, were on the ground floor, and she started down the marble staircase, after a swift look around to make sure that there was no one else about. It might just be possible to appease her hunger without having to appear at the breakfast table.

She was no more than half-way down the stairs, however, when she heard the sound of a door closing somewhere, and a moment later someone called her from the gallery. 'Miss Gavin!'

Turning swiftly, she looked up at the dark, enquiring face of Alexei Romano and half smiled, her fingers curling instinctively into her palms at the sight of him. 'Good morning, Signor Romano!'

'Are you going out?'

She shook her head, unwilling to tell him that she had been bent on seeking food from the kitchen rather than sit at the breakfast table with him and his household. 'No, *signore*, I was—I was——'

'We always breakfast on the terrace. You do not know the way?'

Why did he never let her finish a sentence? It was no use trying to lie to him and she certainly had no intention of telling him the truth, so she merely shrugged—a Latin gesture that she was beginning to find increasingly useful.

In a moment he was beside her on the stairs, one hand under her arm, his palm warm on her bare flesh, sending that inevitable tingling sensation through her as she walked beside him down the rest of the stairs.

'I will introduce you to the two ladies,' he told her. 'It is as well I caught up with you. Paolo, I suppose, is not down yet.'

'I—I don't think so. I haven't seen anything of him.'

Her expression must have betrayed how she felt at the prospect of meeting the two women, for he looked down at her with a small frown of curiosity, but said nothing for the moment. It was when they stepped down on to the cool tiled floor of the hall that he gripped his fingers round her arm and brought them both to a standstill, and she looked up enquiringly to see a half smile softening the stern lines of his mouth.

'What is it that troubles you?' he asked, and Storm shook her head hastily.

'I—I just feel rather as if—as if I'm being led to the slaughter,' she confessed, again visualising a feminine form of him, and trembling at the prospect.

'So?' The strong fingers tightened their hold, digging into her soft flesh. 'You are not being thrown to the lions, *signorina*. We no longer throw our slaves to the wild beasts to be torn to pieces for our amusement. Have no fear!'

It was a studied and deliberate reference to her rash accusation of yesterday, and she looked up at him, her green eyes reproachful, trying to stop the quite alarming force with which her heart beat at her ribs. It was confusing how the touch of his hand could play such havoc with her emotions and at the same time reassure her.

'I'm nervous enough, Signor Romano,' she told him, her mouth pursed softly. 'There's no need for you to try and make me more so.'

'I did not intend to.' He looked down at her for a moment in silence, his hold on her easing, the fingers moving slowly and soothingly on her arm and playing havoc with her senses. Then the chiselled features softened into a smile again briefly. 'No one will eat you, I promise!'

'That's what Paolo promised about you!' Storm

retorted without thinking. 'And I'm not sure I believe either of you!'

Blue eyes regarded her steadily for a moment, the caressing movement of his fingers stilled again. 'You may believe us both with confidence, Miss Gavin. But I do not relish the idea of being discussed by you with members of my family, especially in a derogatory manner.'

'Oh, but we weren't——'

Her words were cut short when he put a hand under her chin suddenly, raising her face sharply, his fingers spread to hold her firmly while she bore the scrutiny of those blue eyes with a fluttering sensation of panic.

'Always you argue with me,' he said softly, as if the fact both annoyed and intrigued him. 'No one else argues with me, *signorina*, not if they are wise. Why do you persist in doing so?'

'Because I don't think any man has the right to absolute power over others!' She spoke far more bravely than she felt, and with one hand tried to release her chin from that iron grip. 'Please don't hold me like that, you're hurting me!'

A small, tight smile touched his lips for a moment and deliberately the fingers tightened their hold briefly before releasing her. 'I could hurt you much more,' he said, soft-voiced. 'Remember that, *signorina*, hmm?'

Storm made no reply, but rubbed gently at the marks his fingers had left on her skin, her eyes wary and puzzled. 'Signor——'

'You *will* have the last word, will you not?'

He gave her no time to retort to that one, but took her arm again and led her across the hall, under the gaze of those erotic creatures of fantasy that smiled down at them from the painted walls.

The double doors in front of them led into the big room she had seen on her first visit, she knew, but he did not go straight in, instead he stopped again, one hand on the ornate gold handle, looking down at her steadily. She gasped in audible surprise a second later when the soft, deep sound of laughter startled her into stillness.

'You look so much as if you expect to be devoured, Miss Gavin, and I assure you it is not so.' For what seemed like an eternity he studied her in a way that set her pulses racing wildly, and she almost cried out when he reached out and touched her face gently where the grip of his fingers still tingled on her skin. 'I suppose I may not call you Storm, as Paolo does?' he suggested softly, but gave her no time to reply before he shrugged and shook his head. 'Come! Let us go in.'

Storm was trembling as she walked across that big, beautiful room again, sinking into the deep pile of the carpet, richly woven in red and gold, contrasting with the white walls and that wonderful white marble fireplace she had so admired. She had not noticed last time several paintings around the walls, dark and sombre in contrast to their surroundings, looking down at her with bold dark eyes that reminded her more of Paolo Veronese than the man beside her, although she assumed they were mutual ancestors.

With barely time to glance around her, she was led inexorably towards the wide open french windows and out on to a paved terrace, cool and shaded in the morning sun. The garden smelled fresh and lovely and she could see the glitter of the sea far below, that deep, deep blue as only the Mediterranean can be.

A white wrought-iron table was set for a continental breakfast with coffee, rolls and fine porcelain jars of jam. Already seated at the table were two women, and at the sight of them Storm swallowed hard.

One of them looked just as she had feared they both would. Stern-faced and unbending, if her expression was anything to judge by, dressed in all-enveloping black, despite the warmth of the sun. It was to this unpromising prospect that Alexei Romano took her first.

'This is Miss Gavin, Aunt Sofia.' Thank heaven he introduced her in English. 'Miss Gavin, my aunt, Signora Veronese.'

So this was Paolo's mama! Storm would never have attributed such an extrovert son to this stern, unfriendly woman, except that there was some facial likeness somewhere.

Her black hair was well streaked with grey and drawn back from a face that could never have laid claim to beauty, and yet bore a quite definite resemblance to Paolo's good looks. A tight-lipped mouth, Storm felt, disapproved of almost everyone, there was nothing personal to her in its censure.

'*Signora.*' The hand Storm offered was pointedly ignored, and the unfriendly dark eyes openly suspected her of conniving her way into the villa simply to be near to Paolo. It would never occur to her to suspect that the opposite was the fact.

Storm turned from her with relief, for her companion looked quite another matter. She was already smiling, one long slim hand extended in greeting, when they turned to her, and shrewd but kindly dark eyes welcomed her.

Her hair was so red that it was impossible to suppose that it was other than artificial, but her face, despite some obvious signs of ageing, was still quite lovely, and it, at least, was free of artifice.

'Lisetta!' Alexei Romano leaned over her, one arm lightly about her shoulders in a gesture of affection that surprised Storm. 'This is Miss Gavin, Lisetta. Miss Gavin, the, Contessa Luisa Berenitti.'

'Oh, but, Alexei *caro,* how enchanting!' She winked an eye at Alexei before smiling again at Storm. 'Wecome to our family, Signorina Gavin, we have heard so much about you. *Dio!* But you have caused such—*eccitamento* among our young men! Eh, Alexei?' She used beringed and expressive hands to enlarge her meaning and her eyes rolled as she laughed delightedly. Not for the Contessa the dullness of black; she wore a bright green summer dress that revealed plump bare arms to the shoulders. Her bright curious eyes smiled up at Storm encouragingly. 'You will like being with us, *signorina*?'

Storm nodded, a little overwhelmed by the woman's bold, bright character, but liking her just the same, and thanking heaven that she was such a complete contrast to Paolo's deterring mother. 'I hope so, Contessa.'

'And you are to take care of our *piccolo, si*?' The red head tilted to one side, the bright eyes enquiring. 'He is a charming *bambino*, our Gino, no?'

'He's a dear little boy,' Storm agreed willingly. 'We get along very well together so far.'

'*Bene!* He will adore you too.' Again that uninhibited laugh shrilled out and she glanced at her sober neighbour with wickedly twinkling eyes. 'Like his uncle, *si*?'

Quite forgetting for the moment that Gino also called Paolo his uncle, Storm turned and looked up at Alexei Romano with wide, startled eyes, and to her surprise and dismay saw that the usually icy-blue eyes were warm with laughter.

'Gino also calls Paolo his uncle,' he reminded her softly, and she felt the warm, bright colour flood into her cheeks again. She had never felt such a complete fool in her life, and she supposed that it was inevitable that the one time she had seen Alexei Romano laugh, it had to be at her expense.

The Contessa's dark eyes had missed nothing of the byplay and they flicked from Alexei to Storm swiftly, then she pulled a wry face. 'Oh, but of course I meant Paolo! *Mi spiace, signorina!*'

Sorry or not she was amused by the mistake, and Storm wondered how on earth she could have been so idiotic as to make it. 'Oh, please don't think——' She sought to explain, knowing she had attempted the wrong thing as soon as she spoke. 'It was—I mean I——'

A long finger was laid firmly across her lips and she raised startled eyes to see Alexei Romano shaking his head at her slowly, that warm glimpse of laughter still lingering in his eyes. *'Quieto, po' oca!'* he said softly, and the Contessa smiled.

'You are not yet used to us, *signorina*,' she smiled kindly. 'You will soon accept our ways and forget about being so——' Expressive shoulders consigned her English reserve to the things best forgotten.

Storm liked the Contessa, although she was none the wiser, even now, as to who or what she was to the family, or even if she was one of them. Alexei had given her no other title than Contessa. Whoever she was, Storm decided, she would make a valuable ally in times of stress.

The next few days passed rather like a dream for Storm, although Gino kept her on her toes with his constant barrage of questions about England. He wanted to go there one day, he confided; his Uncle Alexei had been and he liked it.

The latter rather surprised her, for she could not see the English temperament appealing to Alexei Romano at all, unless she had misjudged him badly. Paolo, she knew, had never been to England, for he made much of the fact that he had never been to the country of her birth. Paolo was given to making extravagant and emotional statements like that, and she was learning to take them in her stride, but she still enjoyed hearing them.

He had arranged to take her to see the famous Bay of Naples, and she had breathed a sigh of relief when Gino went to bed without too much fuss, giving her more time to bath and change. She surveyed the result in a long mirror and smiled at the sense of unreality the reflected bedroom always gave her.

The reversed picture of the lace-draped bed and gilt-scrolled ceiling, with the high, curved window, gave even her own reflection a dream-like quality. A sleeveless dress in turquoise blue softly flattered her figure and made her tawny hair look almost gold, and her green eyes almost jade. It was a very pleasant picture altogether.

She swung her shoulder-length hair back from her face and smiled at her reflection. The Italian sun had already given her a soft, glowing tan and she refused to disguise it with make-up so that her skin glowed warmly and naturally.

Leaving her own room at last, she quietly opened Gino's door and found him still looking at the picture book she had left him with. He beamed a smile at her and she opened the door wider and went across to him, shaking her head at him.

'You are going out with Zio Paolo?' he asked, his bright dark eyes approving of her dress and the burnished softness of her hair. There was something disturbingly adult about Gino sometimes that reminded her of Paolo.

'We're just going for a ride,' she told him. 'And I think it's high time you went to sleep, young man.'

He made no objection when she took the book from him but sat curled up in his bed like a little black-eyed gnome, his small gamin-like face bright with mischief and not a bit sleepy. 'Zio Paolo he is——' His hands and expressive rolling eyes conveyed his meaning all too clearly, and as only a Latin could—even one as young as Gino. '*Molto amoroso, si, signorina?*'

'Gino!'

Her voice held a warning note, but she struggled with the laughter that rose to her lips and Gino knew it. 'You like Zio Paolo, *si*?' he insisted, and Storm pulled back the covers and pulled him down in the bed.

'Sleep!' she told him.

'*Si*, Signorina Gavin!' He lay back on his pillows, the light bedclothes up under his chin, and when she turned in the doorway to smile at him, he winked an eye expertly. '*Ciao!*' he said softly, and his black eyes danced wickedly above the edge of the sheet.

The ride along the coast road to Naples was wonderful. The beautiful Amalfi motorway with its breathtaking scenery running all the way from Naples to Salerno, right round the Sorrento peninsula, was well worth a long drive, so Paolo had promised Storm, but this evening they had to make do with the section of it from Bellabaia to Naples.

She had less time to appreciate it than she would have liked because Paolo drove so fast, careering along at a hair-raising speed. There was so much to look at that she was tempted to suggest that he drove a little more slowly, but hesitated to do so.

Acres of citrus groves, oranges, lemons and limes, sweetly scented; apples, pears and peaches too, all grew in this rich fertile soil. Storm had noticed, at intervals, what looked like little straw roofs over the tree tops and asked Paolo about them. He laughed, apparently only too pleased to air his knowledge.

'The *pagliarelle*?'

She cocked her head to one side, not attempting to repeat the name. 'Is that what they are? What are they for?'

'To protect the fruit, *cara mia*, what else?' His smile teased her. 'Even here we can have unexpected bad weather, you know. *Tempesta!* Like you, *bella mia*, only that sort of storm can ruin the harvest!'

Storm gazed up at the clear evening sky, finding it difficult to visualise the weather here as anything but perfect. 'I find it hard to believe it can storm here.'

'Ah, but it is true, *cara*! How else would any-

76

thing grow? We have to have rain sometimes.'

She leaned her head back against the seat and sighed with sheer contentment, feeling more relaxed than she had for days.

The countryside was like one vast orchard, the rich, dark soil producing crop after crop of oranges and lemons, and almost every other fruit imaginable, with neat acres of tomatoes, cauliflowers and onions in between. It was, as she said, too good to be true, a veritable garden of Eden with the wide fast motorway leading inexorably to Naples and the markets of the world.

The road swept along the cliff tops, giving breathtaking glimpses of the deep blue Mediterranean beyond the groves on the cliff face, and beyond those acres of trees on the other side hazy glimpses of hills including the promise of Vesuvius somewhere ahead of them. She could, she felt, have gone on for ever.

Before long, however, the fertile stretches began to give way before the first signs of industry. Heavy industry, crude and stark after the beauty of the previous miles. Fat, round tanks of oil refineries, and towering cranes in shipbuilding yards breaking the skyline instead of trees, gave a quite different character from the picture of Italy as she had visualised it. There was even a cement works with its ubiquitous white dust falling over everything.

It was the new, more ruthless side of the country that she supposed gave Alexei Romano, and others, their immense wealth, but had little appeal for

Storm. It was, however, interesting to discover that so much industry existed in a place she would never have dreamed of expecting it.

She was happier when they left the industrial belt behind them and ran down towards Naples itself. The view from the top of a hill was breathtaking, and every bit as wonderful as she had been led to expect.

The famous bay looked huge and sparkling deep blue in the evening sunshine with terrace upon terrace of little houses, many of them multi-storied and mostly varying shades of white, staggering up into the hills behind the city, with Mount Vesuvius sitting menacingly in the background.

Hot, flamboyant and exciting, all those words came into her mind as she looked down at Naples through a softening robe of trees, and her heart was suddenly beating even more rapidly as Paolo took the car plunging down towards it, creating a fresh cool breeze saltily moist from the sea.

'It—wonderful!'

Paolo turned his head briefly and looked at her, smiling and well pleased with her reaction. He took the car into the side of the road, a rather hazardous thing to do on such a road, and braked to a halt high above the city. 'So,' he said softly. 'You like Napoli, yes?'

'It looks marvellous!'

'Shall we go down?' His dark eyes were warmly persuasive and she mentally hardened her heart to resist the inevitable plea. 'We could go to a night club, *cara mia*. Dance a little, maybe a little—*romanza, si?*'

'I don't think so, Paolo.' She still had Alexei Romano's warning in mind, about getting back at a reasonable hour and how Paolo would probably persuade her otherwise. But the hint of hesitation in her voice was her undoing.

Paolo leaned across and touched her cheek lightly with a caressing finger. 'Why are you so afraid to come with me, *bellissima?*'

'I'm not afraid,' Storm denied, smiling despite the flutter in her heart. Paolo might not have his cousin's forceful magnetism, but he was pretty effective in his own right, and very hard to resist.

'Afraid of Alexei, then?'

His eyes challenged her to deny it and she hastily lowered her gaze, unwilling to debate that point. 'Not exactly afraid,' she told him. 'But I do have to mind my p's and q's, Paolo.'

'Your——' He dismissed the unfamiliar phrase with the inevitable shrug, intent on persuading her. 'Forget about Alexei. Come and dance with me, *carissima*, hmm?'

It was inevitable, of course, and Storm sighed as she yielded. 'All right, Paolo,' she said. 'I'll come and dance.'

'*Bene!*' He leaned across and kissed her lightly on her mouth, content to have got his way.

Down in the city itself, the life and bustle in the teeming streets was almost overwhelming, but Storm was carried along on the tide of excited and good-natured banter that followed their progress through the narrow streets from the waterfront.

It was the old Naples she was seeing, a city of rich, florid buildings, heavily and almost rakishly endowed with rich carvings and fluted columns, reaching up above the narrow streets to the clear blue sky. Some of them were shabby with age, some slowly decaying, but still impressive, beautiful and used.

Even the tall, once proud *palazzos,* which had housed the wealthy and influential of another age, now gave shelter to whole families in their vast basement rooms. Families who lived close and called vociferously and cheerfully to one another in friendly argument.

It was a noisy, bright and overcrowded maze of history and humanity, and Paolo seemed to know every inch of it, driving the big car down small streets that Storm would never have dared venture along.

Presently, however, he took them to a much newer part, where the houses and shops were modern and much less impressive. The new Naples, Paolo told her, and it entered her head that they could have been in almost any city in the world. She had little time to lose interest, however, for he turned into a car park suddenly and smilingly helped her out of the car.

The night club was garish and noisy, and she was not altogether happy about being there, but Paolo seemed to be known there and he was quite happy about it, so she made no comment. Whatever she felt about her surroundings, she had no complaint about her escort, for Paolo was, as always, attentive and flattering, very good for her ego and the target of a number of interested feminine eyes. The noise made her head ache, but with such an escort she had not the heart to ask him to take her home.

They were driving along the motorway, on the way back, before she fully realised how late they were, and she bit on her lip anxiously when she thought about Alexei Romano. 'It's nearly two o'clock, Paolo,' she said, and he shrugged carelessly.

'So—does it matter, *cara*?'

'It does,' Storm told him. 'I have orders to be in at a reasonable time, and I'm quite sure Signor Romano won't call two o'clock in the morning a reasonable hour.'

'Orders?' He laughed shortly. '*Madre di Dio!* Alexei can be quite—feudal!'

'I had noticed,' Storm said wryly. 'I said as much to him once and almost lost my job.'

'*Si?*' He flicked her a brief glance, his eyes almost luminous in the bright moonlight, then he shrugged. 'It is his Russian mama, of course. I do not remember Aunt Natasha very well, she went off and left them when Alexei was still a little boy, but she was very—Russian! Gloomy and stern, *comprende*?'

'Oh, I see, he's half Russian!' She nodded her head in understanding, her questions about his unusual features answered at last. 'I wondered. There had to be something to account for those blue eyes and that wonderful bone structure.'

She did wonder if she had been a little too effusive, and Paolo's next words confirmed it. 'Which the ladies find irresistible,' he declared with a surprising hint of envy, and Storm looked surprised.

'Do they?' Somehow she had not thought of Alexei Romano as a ladies' man despite his incredible attraction.

'He does not notice, or so he pretends!' He shrugged resignedly and Storm almost laughed aloud.

'Well, I don't think you have much to complain about in that direction, Paolo!'

'No, we have our share of good looks in the Romano family.' He spoke without a trace of false modesty and she smiled to herself. Paolo was really quite refreshingly honest. 'My mama was a Romano, of course. She and Alexei's father were brother and sister.'

'Oh, I see.' She pondered on that for a moment as they sped through the cool moonlit night, with the scents of the citrus groves heady and sweet around them. 'You're not very much alike, are you? You and Alexei?'

'No, no, I suppose not.' He made the admission with a shrug. 'Alexei thinks of nothing but the business—except for his precious racehorses, of course. He's so mad about them that he even helps to exercise them when he has time.'

So that explained another mystery about Alexei

Romano, she thought. Why he had been wearing riding clothes when she first met him. She was learning quite a bit about her employer tonight. It seemed there were any number of facets to that complicated character, and most of them intriguing.

CHAPTER FIVE

IT was a quarter past two when Paolo let them into the villa, and Storm felt terribly guilty, although he had assured her that it was not very late by his standards, and since Alexei knew she was out with him he would surely not expect her very early either.

It was very silent in that big, ornate hall and the tiled floor whispered under Storm's light shoes as she crossed to the stairs. The lights were still on, but she was not sure that they did not stay all night, so it did not surprise her too much. What did surprise her, however, and made her gasp audibly was to hear herself called as she prepared to follow Paolo up the stairs.

'*Signorina!*'

The one word in that harsh cold voice brought her to an immediate and abrupt halt, her eyes wide and wary as she turned. She had no doubt who called her even before she saw Alexei Romano's tall figure in the doorway of the sitting-room, and she wanted Paolo out of the way before he became involved in whatever his cousin had in mind for her.

'I'll see you in the morning,' she whispered to him. 'Goodnight, Paolo!'

'But, *cara*——'

'*Please*, Paolo!'

His instinctive gallantry made him want to stay and lend her his support, but the sight of his cousin's dark features set so sternly made him doubt the wisdom, and with Storm's anxiety to send him away so obvious he at last made up his mind. The inevitable shrug both recognised her reasons and apologised for not staying, and he continued on up the stairs.

The tall figure in the light suit had stepped back into the room and Storm sighed deeply as she turned from watching Paolo depart and walked across the hall. He stood in front of the huge fireplace, dark and menacing, his hands behind his back, that square chin thrust out aggressively, and when she came into the room he looked pointedly at his wristwatch.

'Is two-fifteen in the morning your idea of a reasonable hour, *signorina*?' His voice was as cold as the ice-blue eyes that looked at her, daring her to offer a defence.

Storm felt a shiver run through her, suddenly cold after the long cool drive, and she put a hand to cover the top of her arm, shrugging her shoulders protectively. 'I—I didn't realise how late it was, Signor Romano.'

'No doubt in my cousin's company you lost all sense of time!'

The hint of sarcasm brought a glitter of resentment to her green eyes, but she managed to keep her voice steady, although she was conscious as always of the churning sense of excitement he aroused in her. Her heart was thudding heavily and a pulse at her temple fluttered warningly.

'No, *signore*.'

'Were you then delayed by an accident?'

'No, Signor Romano, I purely and simply didn't notice the time.' She looked at him as steadily as her chaotic emotions allowed. 'I'm sorry if you think I've been—remiss, but I did see Gino safely into bed before I left, and I was under the impression that I had done all that was required of me for the day.'

'So?' The ice-blue eyes condemned her without mercy. 'I have to inform you, *signorina*, that less than an hour ago Gino was calling for you! He had a—bad dream, he has them quite often since his parents were killed, and he was very distressed that you were not there.'

'Oh, I'm so sorry!'

There seemed little else she could say in the circumstances, although she could see that he considered it no excuse for her absence. 'If you had been here at a reasonable hour as I instructed you to be, you would have been able to deal with it.'

'I'm——'

'As it was, fortunately I heard him calling when I went up to my room, or he would have been even more distressed. No one else can hear him when he calls.'

That was true enough, she knew, for Gino's room was between her own and his uncle's and only the two of them were close enough to hear a cry. 'I'm sorry. I really *am* sorry, *signore*. But——' She hesitated to voice any criticism in the circumstances, but he could not deny the truth of what she had to say. 'You could have warned me about Gino having nightmares, Signor Romano.'

'It would have made a difference?'

The cold eyes dared her to confirm it, but she nodded vehemently. 'Yes, of course it would!' He looked as if he was in two minds whether or not to believe her. 'Now I know,' she went on determinedly, 'I can arrange to always be back at a reasonable time.'

'Good!' He nodded sharply. 'I am glad that at last I have managed to impress upon you the importance of your duties. That you are here to care for Gino and not to amuse Paolo until the early hours of the morning!'

Storm could feel her heart racing wildly as anger and frustration battled for precedence. Why would he always believe the worst of her? 'You have no right to say that, Signor Romano!' She curled her hands, tightly, into fists at her sides, her eyes shining like green jewels in her flushed face as she defied him.

To her surprise he did not immediately put her sharply in her place, but merely stood there looking down at her, tense and alert, a small nerve at the base of his throat throbbing rapidly. 'Always you defy me, argue with me,' he said softly, at last. 'Will you never learn, *signorina*?'

87

'That you own me body and soul because I work for you, *signore*?' She stuck out her chin, angry enough to be uncaring. 'You don't, Signor Romano! No one does!'

'Perhaps that is a pity!' The blue eyes, she noticed with a start, were no longer icy but dark and shadowed with some emotion that was betrayed too in the slight huskiness of his voice. The way he stood, with his feet slightly apart, as usual, his hands behind his back, the open neck of his shirt revealing the muscular brown throat. Every nerve in his body seemed tensed, and she felt a flicker of fear for a moment when he moved suddenly.

She stepped back instinctively, her left hand still covering the top of her right arm, hugging herself against the chill she had felt earlier, although she was glowingly warm now. He noted the instinctive move and for a moment his eyes blazed at her, as if it angered him further, then he smiled. A small, tight and quite humourless smile that did nothing to reassure her.

'Do you judge me by Paolo's standards, *signorina*?'

Storm shook her head, uncertain for a moment just what to do or say, then she realised suddenly what he was implying and shook her head more vehemently. 'Oh no, Signor Romano, I know you have no other interests but your factory! I would not expect you to behave as Paolo would!'

She had barely time to register the blaze of anger

in his eyes before he reached for her suddenly and pulled her against him, his arms hard and tight as steel bands, holding her so close she could feel the fast, steady beat of his heart. His mouth was hard, ruthless and passionately angry, and she would have cried out if she could.

He took no notice of her ineffective struggles but pressed her against his lean hardness as if he wanted to hurt her, and she stopped at last, only pressing her hands against his chest, submitting to the head-spinning chaos of emotions that filled her with both fear and elation.

When he released her at last, she did not stop to consider how she felt, what he would do next, but ran as fast as she could, out of the room and up the wide marble staircase without pausing. In the quiet of her own room, she stood for several seconds with her back leaned against the door, her breathing noisy and erratic, one hand to her head, her legs feeling oddly weak and trembly.

Why had she run? She sought an answer as she walked to the lace-draped bed and sat down on it, pulling off her shoes and dropping them on to the carpet. She had never run from Paolo when he kissed her, but then she had always more or less expected it from Paolo. Alexei Romano was another matter.

She had told him that she would not expect such behaviour from him, implied that he was not capable of it, and apparently he had resented it, more than she anticipated. She would not have run, she felt sure, if he had kissed her in the same spirit that Paolo did. But it had been anger that prompted him, not affection, or admiration, as it was with Paolo, and Storm felt strangely bruised, in spirit as well as in body.

'You are finding us quite easy to live with, Signorina Gavin?' The Contessa's dark and mischievous eyes smiled at Storm across the dinner table, and Storm responded as she always did to the Contessa.

'I'm learning, Contessa.' The brief glance she gave at Alexei Romano at the head of the table was instinctive rather than deliberate. 'After three weeks, I think I'm beginning to fit into the routine now.'

'*Bene!*' The Contessa too looked at Alexei, and one fine brow arched briefly. 'You have chosen well for our Gino, *caro mio*. Signorina Gavin is no—how do you say, *signorina*?—country mouse, huh?'

Storm smiled. 'There is such an expression, Contessa, but it's a misconception to apply it to all English girls.'

'But of course,' the Contessa agreed. 'It is simply that a friend of mine had an English girl too, to take care of her *bambini*, and she was—oooh! *Madre di Dio!*' The expressive hands added meaning to her words. 'She was such a *mouse*, that girl!'

The hard, sharp eyes of Signora Veronese expressed disagreement even before she spoke, and Storm could have guessed that she would be at variance with the Contessa's view. She always was, whenever possible, and it seemed to amuse rather than annoy the Contessa.

'If you are referring to the nurse of the Baldonis',' she said, in her rather stilted English, 'she was of excellent character, Lisetta, and not seeking to further her own cause as so many of her countrywomen are in such a position.'

It was not the first time that Storm had been the target for the Signora's acid implications and she supposed it would not be the last, but she caught Paolo's eyes on her and half smiled at the wry face he pulled, out of his mother's sight. The Contessa, however, was never prepared to let injustice pass without comment and she made some remark in Italian which Storm could not understand, but which brought a flush of dark, angry colour to Signora Veronese's face.

For the moment her venom was redirected at the Contessa and Storm took time to consider why the two women continued to live in the same house when they so obviously disliked one another. In the Signora's case, of course it was, as her son had quite blatantly admitted, because they would be very poor without Alexei Romano's assistance, but it was more difficult to understand why the Contessa remained.

Even after three weeks at the villa, Storm had been unable to discover just where she fitted into the family tree, and she would not have dreamed of asking, no matter how curious she was. She liked the Contessa, even more so now that she knew her better, and she had the strangest feeling that it would embarrass her to have her status in the household defined too explicitly.

While Storm had been preoccupied with her own thoughts she was aware that a conversation was going on in Italian, but it was one sharp, unmistakable word, spat out by Signora Veronese, that brought her back sharply to earth. The Signora's face was darkly flushed and her black eyes glared viciously across the table at the Contessa, who was at the moment reaching across to put a soothing hand on Alexei's arm.

'*No*, Alexei *caro, per favor. Lei è molto gentile, ma*——' The eloquent shoulders dismissed the insult as unimportant, although it was obvious that Alexei was less ready to allow it, and his dark brows were drawn together as he looked at his aunt sternly.

'Zia Sofia!'

Storm knew that cold stern voice well enough, and she could almost find it in her heart to pity Signora Veronese, even though she had insulted the Contessa. Alexei in that angry mood was enough to deter anyone, even the Signora, it seemed, for after a moment the sharp black eyes were hastily lowered.

'*Mi spiace*, Lisetta.' The apology was reluctant and made with bad grace, but it was made, and the Contessa was the first to recover her temper. She smiled at Storm and made a moue of apology.

'We are very rude to speak in Italian, Signorina

Gavin, please forgive us. But'—she shrugged again —'it was perhaps as well, hmm?' The shrill but very infectious laugh warmed the chill atmosphere. 'If one is to be insulted, it is as well to be so in one's own language, *si*?'

She was a really remarkable woman, Storm thought, and willingly enough joined the Contessa when she signed that she should do so, as they rose from the table. She gave a hasty glance at her charge, but saw that he was quite happy for the moment with his uncle and followed the Contessa to the cool of the garden.

The breeze was cool and refreshing blowing in from the sea and the scent of the lemons mingled with that of roses was sweet and heady, as they walked beneath the trees, in silence for a moment or two. Then the Contessa turned and looked at Storm, her red head tipped to one side, in an oddly birdlike pose.

'You do not speak any Italian at all, Signorina Gavin?'

Storm shook her head. 'No, Contessa, I'd like to learn, but I don't have much time really.'

'Ah, *si*!' Those expressive eyes rolled wickedly. 'Paolo is busy teaching you other things, eh?' She laughed uninhibitedly, as always. 'You should ask Alexei, *cara mia*, I am sure he would be very pleased to help you learn our language.'

'I'm sure he wouldn't!' Storm laughed, without giving much thought to the impression she was giving, and the Contessa looked at her shrewdly for a moment.

'You do not think that Alexei has time for such things?' she asked, and Storm hesitated for a moment before replying.

'I doubt if he would consider teaching me Italian was very worthwhile, Contessa. Signor Romano does not—well, he doesn't altogether approve of me—most of the time.'

'Ah! But the rest of the time, *piccola*!' She put a wealth of meaning into her eyes and Storm could feel the colour in her cheeks, something that seemed to delight the Contessa, who smiled broadly.

'I work for Signor Romano, that's all,' Storm said firmly. 'That's *all*, Contessa!'

Her very vehemence seemed to convince the Contessa that there was something more than that, and she nodded her head. 'You are a very beautiful young woman, Signorina—Storm, *si*?' Storm nodded with a smile. 'You misjudge my Alexei if you think he is any more the blind man than Sofia's Paolo!'

'But, Contessa——'

'Ah, no, no! I am right, you will see.'

Storm could not help remembering that kiss, some two weeks ago when she had come home very late with Paolo, but that had been prompted by anger not—whatever it was the Contessa had in mind, and she hoped no one else had similar thoughts on the same subject.

'You like Paolo?'

The question sounded far more than merely idle

curiosity and Storm looked at her for a moment, then nodded. 'I like Paolo very much, Contessa, but there is nothing serious there, either.' She smiled wryly. 'With Paolo it would be foolish to expect there could be!'

A long slim hand was laid gently on her arm and the red head nodded approvingly. 'I am glad you can see that, *cara*. Sofia would never allow it.' She pulled a dismal face and shrugged those eloquent shoulders again. 'When Paolo marries, it will be someone with—how is it? Much money.'

It was a little embarrassing being the receiver of such confidences, but Storm supposed that the family took such matters in their stride. Paolo had admitted himself that he and his mother were very poor, or would be without Alexei's help, and it would be accepted as quite logical for him to marry a wealthy girl, when one could be found who would turn a blind eye to Paolo's past record.

'I suppose marriages are arranged still sometimes?' she ventured, and the Contessa laughed shortly, the bitterest sound Storm had ever heard her make.

'Ah, *si, si, piccola mia*! They are more easily made than undone!'

'Of course.' She remembered that divorce was not the easy matter in Italy that it was in most of the rest of the world.

They walked in silence for a while, then the Contessa smiled at her, one hand reaching out to touch her arm again. 'I like you, Storm, *cara mia*,

95

you—how is it? Listen well?'

'A good listener,' Storm smiled, and the Contessa nodded. '*Si*, a good listener.' She said nothing else for several minutes again, then spoke more slowly, as if she sought for the right words. 'You wonder who it is that I am, is that not so, Storm?'

'Oh no, I——'

The red head was shaking vehemently. 'It is so, *cara*, I know. You cannot think if I am an—aunt? Or what I am to my Alexei, no?' She did not wait for confirmation, taking it for granted. 'Did you know that his mama went away when he was a little boy?'

'Yes,' Storm admitted. 'Paolo did tell me that.'

'But no more, eh?' She smiled gently. 'He is much more the soft heart than his mama.' Storm remembered that word spat out so viciously at the dinner table, but said nothing. 'In some way it was my fault that Signora Romano left her two little boys, *cara*. I was to blame, only partly, you will understand, but—*si*, I was to blame.'

'You were?' Storm stared at her uncertainly. 'But——'

'She was a—a woman of no laughter, you understand? And I was——' Those expressive shoulders described her own more youthful image as clearly as any words could have done. 'I was the cause, but yet who can blame a man if he seeks laughter and a happy face? She went away, and the two little boys needed a mother. I adored them and they liked me —my *bambini*. No!' She shook her head sharply, her dark eyes suddenly misted as she remembered. 'Now there is only Alexei!'

'And you never——' It was difficult to know just what to say after such confidences, but the dark eyes showed only sorrow for her foster-son, no resentment. She shrugged resignedly. 'As you will know, *cara*, marriages are made to last in Italy, and the Signora is still alive.'

'Of course—I'm sorry.'

'Ah, *si, piccola mia*, you too have the soft heart, more so even than Paolo, I think, but you must not feel sorry for me, *bimba*. I had some happy times with Luigi and my boys!' A long gentle hand lay on Storm's arm for a moment. 'If one has love, there are many things one can face.' That bright, rather shrill laughter shattered the stillness of the garden for a moment. 'Even the scorn of Sofia!' She shook her head slowly, her eyes sad again, the expressive, mobile face uncharacteristically bitter. 'Poor Gina, she was not so—able.'

'Gina?' The name told Storm most of what she wanted to know, and the Contessa's words confirmed it.

'Our little Gino's mama, *cara*. She was very beautiful, but'—another telling shrug—'Benito had less sense of what is right than Alexei. Alexei would have married her.'

So Gino was not a Romano, Storm thought ruefully. Poor Gino, as bereft of social standing as the Contessa, and yet safely housed under Alexei Romano's roof, as she was. It seemed as if every soul in the house owed Alexei Romano their love and gratitude, but only half of them really gave it.

'Gino's adorable,' she said, more to try and lighten the sudden air of sadness that had descended on them than for any other reason.

The Contessa smiled. 'He is *poco folletto, si?* And he is very lucky little boy too, I think. Alexei loves him like a son, he would—how is it?—adopt him one day, so that he can be a Romano.'

'Oh, but that would be——'

'Signorina Gavin!'

The cool, familiar voice cut across her words, and she turned, a faint and disturbing sense of guilt making her flush when she looked into Alexei's light eyes. 'Yes, Signor Romano?'

'Gino is waiting for you.' He came across towards them, his footsteps deadened on the softness of grass, the stern lines of his face softened by the shadows thrown by the trees.

He had changed into a shirt that was almost the same ice blue as his eyes and open at the neck, showing a deep vee of strong brown throat and that soft, throbbing pulse at the base of it. As always when he came near her, Storm felt her fingers curl instinctively into her palms, and she was aware of the Contessa's dark eyes watching her shrewdly.

'I'll go to him,' she said hastily, and moved off immediately, making a wide detour so as not to pass too close to him.

Quickly as she moved, it was not fast enough to avoid hearing the Contessa's rather carrying voice, scolding her foster-son gently, 'Oh, Alexei, *caro mio!*' And she had no difficulty in imagining that vivid red head shaking reproachfully.

Storm lay in her bed, too hot to get to sleep, thinking about the lovely evening she had had with Paolo, and thanking heaven that she had managed this time to get him to bring them home at a reasonable hour, despite his dislike of the idea.

She had been out with Paolo quite often since the night four weeks ago when they had returned to the villa at two o'clock in the morning to find Alexei waiting for her, but each time it had been far later than she liked, and each time she had prayed that Gino would not have another disturbed night, and Alexei would find her wanting in her duties as nurse.

That night was firmly fixed in her mind, and she told herself that she had no wish to repeat any part of the experience, although if she was quite honest, she was not sure whether she entirely believed it.

She enjoyed going out and about with Paolo, partly because he was very good for her ego, and partly because he was such excellent company and made her laugh a lot. Also, for some perverse reason she could not quite explain, she liked to see that faint frown that sometimes appeared on Alexei's uncompromising features when Paolo chattered at the table about their outings. Neither Alexei nor Signora Veronese altogether approved of their outings, she felt.

Quite often she found herself wondering what Alexei Romano would say about some of the things they did and the places they went to. He never passed comment, but she sometimes suspected he was tempted to, and the possibility of his one day doing so intrigued her without her quite knowing why.

She raised her head from the pillows suddenly when she thought she heard a faint cry from Gino's room. He had been safely asleep when she looked in on him before she came to bed, but he could have woken, and she must go to him if he called out.

Only once in the four weeks since that night had he had another nightmare and then, fortunately, she had been back and no one but her the wiser. Another cry confirmed her suspicions, and in a minute she was out of bed and reaching for her robe, pulling the soft, pink, silky material round her shoulders and tying the sash as she went.

Another cry, this time louder and more urgent, and she opened the door of Gino's room, turning on the overhead light as she came in. 'Gino!' He sat up in his bed, a tiny pathetic figure with tears rolling down his face and his huge eyes wide with some already half-forgotten fear, not really awake, nor asleep, but in a no-man's-land of fear, and seeking comfort.

He reached out his arms to her as she came near, and she sat on the edge of the bed, hugging him close, rocking gently and soothingly, a hand on his

head. 'It's all right, Gino, it's all right,' she consoled him in a whisper. 'Don't cry any more, *piccolo*. Sssh, *caro mio*!' The Italian words came instinctively to her tongue as she consoled him, and
he clung to her tightly for a moment, his hands hot
and anxious, his body shaken with sobs, until
gradually he quietened.

'Gino?'

She had left the door ajar when she came into
the room and she started nervously when someone
spoke behind her. A tall, dark figure stood in the
doorway, a deep red silk robe tied carelessly about
his waist and revealing a bare muscular chest.
Storm looked across at him and immediately felt
her heartbeat speed up rapidly as she met his
anxious gaze.

'What is wrong?' he asked, and she shook her
head, her face resting gently against Gino's black
head.

'Gino had a bad dream,' she explained, soft-
voiced, because Gino had not stirred, and she wondered if he was already half asleep again. 'It's all
right, Signor Romano.'

'I heard him cry out.'

His room was on the other side of Gino's, so it
was quite feasible that he had been disturbed as
easily as she had herself. She wondered too, if he
had thought to check on her and make sure she was
with Gino. 'He was frightened.' She rocked Gino
gently in her arms, not daring to look at him when
he came and stood beside them, in an oddly pro-

tective attitude.

'One feels so——' The broad shoulders shrugged, but not carelessly; rather as if he wished he could take whatever was troubling Gino on to his own broad back, and Storm felt a sudden exquisite agony of tenderness for both the man and the boy.

'He'll be all right now,' she said softly, one hand still soothing Gino's hair. 'I'm sorry he disturbed you, Signor Romano.'

'How could you help it?'

The question was reasonable enough, she supposed, but yet she felt bound to apologise, because he held her responsible for Gino's welfare and she had once fallen short of what was expected of her. 'I couldn't,' she whispered back. 'But I thought you were probably asleep.'

She cradled the little figure gently in her arms still, and tried not to notice how the ice-blue eyes of the man took note of her tousled hair and the flimsy softness of her robe and nightgown. 'Were you not also asleep?' he asked, and she shook her head.

'It's too hot. I'm not used to it yet, and I closed the window earlier because it seemed cooler, now I can't open it again.'

'It is never closed at this time of year,' he told her, and she smiled inwardly at the hint of criticism in his voice, even at a moment like this.

'Well, perhaps I shouldn't have touched it then, but I did feel a bit chill earlier.'

'Is he asleep?' He looked down at his nephew,

bending to peer at the dark little face close to her breast, and bringing his own face much too close for comfort so that she felt her pulses respond as they always did.

'I think so.' She moved Gino gently back against her arm and looked down at the small face with his eyes fast closed, the remains of those fat rolling tears still on his cheeks. She gently brushed them away with a fingertip before laying him back on to his pillow. 'It soon passes if there's someone to re-assure them.'

'And he trusts you.'

She pulled the covers carefully over the sleeping boy, so as not to disturb him, and also to delay having to straighten up and find herself close beside Alexei Romano. Her pulses were thudding heavily at her ribs and her temple, and she could feel that taut sense of excitement that he always seemed to generate.

It was instinct, too, that made her bend and kiss the little boy's face before she left him, straightening up swiftly when she felt a hand on her arm. Turning away from the bed, the back of her fingers brushed the softness of silk and she shivered when the warmth of his body burned her through the thin material.

He walked just behind her to the door and it was he who turned off the light, leaving them in the dim softness of the wall light on the gallery. 'Good-night, *signore*.' She would have turned and gone back to her own room, but he was still beside her when she reached her door and she looked up at him wide-eyed and startled.

'Your window must be opened if you are to sleep,' he told her, keeping his voice low, and she looked at him for a moment, scarcely able to believe that he was offering to perform the service himself.

'Oh, it—it doesn't matter really,' she whispered. 'I can manage if I stand on a chair or something; it's just the top of it that's stuck, that's all.'

'I will not allow you to damage yourself or whatever it is you would choose to stand on,' he informed her firmly, and that familiar chiselled look hardened his features putting paid to any argument she may have raised. 'I will open the window for you, then there will be no fear of broken legs, either yours or one of the chairs.'

The ice-blue eyes dared her to read any other reason into his offer to help and eventually she nodded, opening her door and holding the neck of her robe close up under her chin. 'Thank you, *signore*,' she said demurely.

He strode across the room with an air of familiarity that seemed to establish his claim to everything in it, and Storm watched as he reached the top of the obstinate window easily, without the aid of a chair or anything else. He hit it hard with the heel of his hand, then pushed it open as far as it would go, letting in the cooler air from the garden.

In the short time it took him to do all that, she studied him. Noticing the way the silk robe clung to the lean, muscular length of his body, and the strong bare brown legs that showed from the knees down. Judging by what was revealed top and bottom of the robe, she thought it unlikely that he wore anything at all under it.

'Is that right for you?'

He swung round and looked at her, so suddenly that she shook her head hastily to clear it, her lips parted in surprise, caught unawares. 'Oh! Oh yes! Thank you, *signore*!'

'*Bene!* Now perhaps you will sleep.'

'Thank you very much.'

The blue eyes looked at her for a moment while he still stood by the window, and she would have sworn that she saw a glimpse of laughter in their depths. 'That is the third time that you have thanked me, *signorina*,' he said softly. 'The service was really far too small to warrant such effusion!'

'I—I'm sorry.'

She dared not look at him again, and she instinctively held her hands tightly together in front of her when she heard him walk across the room. He stopped in front of her and she could feel the increasing beat of her heart, alarmingly conscious of the way he was looking down at her.

Her soft tawny hair was tumbled from the pillows, and her lightly tanned skin softly flushed with pink. She stood there not knowing what to do or what to say, but increasingly aware of him as a man, and of the deep surge of excitement he aroused in her.

'Would it worry you as much if it was Paolo who was here with you?' he asked softly then, and Storm looked up at him wide-eyed and reproachful.

'Paolo would never come into my room!' she denied firmly.

'Indeed he would, if you allowed him to.' The light eyes speculated as they looked down at her, and she suddenly felt herself growing angry when she suspected he was trying to trap her into an admission of some sort.

'I have no intention of allowing him to, Signor Romano!'

'Of course not.'

She looked up at him suspiciously, her green eyes glowing. She had no reason to think he was being sarcastic, but her senses were alert to every hint, every word he said, and she chose to read sarcasm into his denial whether he intended it or not.

'At least Paolo wouldn't come into my room without an invitation, *signore*! You wouldn't be here if you hadn't taken it upon yourself to come in. I didn't invite you!'

For a moment she had the wild idea that he might hit her, for the icy eyes blazed at her furiously. His reasons for coming to her room had been perfectly innocent, she felt sure, with only the intention of helping her, and by implying otherwise she had made him angry. The last thing she wanted to do.

'Very well, Miss Gavin!' He bowed his dark head briefly and managed to make it both dignified and autocratic, despite his unconventional garb. 'Please forgive me for compromising you. Goodnight!'

'Oh!' Storm watched him as far as the door then, for some quite inexplicable reason, ran after him and put a hand on his arm, her heart fluttering wildly when she touched him. 'Please, Signor Romano, I—I didn't mean—I mean I'm grateful to you for opening the window for me, but I——'

He said nothing for a long moment, and Storm was shaking like a leaf while he stood there looking down at her, that irresistible excitement he generated reaching out to envelop her until she could have cried out. Then, without a word, he reached out his hands and pulled her into his arms, the unbelievable strength of him leaving her no will of her own as he crushed her against him.

His mouth was hard and demanding, angry and hurtful, as it had been last time, but she made no effort to break free for several moments, merely submitting to the wild and quite irresistible excitement that coursed through her. Then, suddenly, she became aware of some faint, almost indistinguishable sound from outside in the gallery, and realised with a flick of panic that someone else was about, and that her bedroom door was wide open.

Alexei Romano too had heard whatever it was, and in a moment he released her and strode to the doorway, looking along the dimly lit gallery, but apparently seeing no one. He looked back at her suddenly, and the ice-blue eyes were darkly shadowed, so that she instinctively shivered when she lowered her own hastily.

'My apologies, Miss Gavin.' He bobbed his head briefly again in dismissal. 'Goodnight!'

Storm stood there for several seconds, her hands to her breast, her mind clear of sleep and whirling chaotically, and this time she did not call him back.

CHAPTER SIX

It was Paolo who made the first mention of Alexei's indiscretion, after dinner the following day. Paolo and Alexei were seldom in at lunch-time, but had their meal at the works; an idea that Paolo was not very enthusiastic about, but was wise enough not to say so within his cousin's hearing.

It had struck Storm at lunch-time that Signora Veronese looked rather smug, and the change of face rather troubled her, although she could not have said why. The Contessa had noticed the change, she thought, too, and would probably extract the reason for it when the opportunity arose. It was silly of Storm to bother, of course, but with Alexei Romano's visit to her room still so vivid in her mind, she supposed she felt a little guilty and more sensitive than usual.

After dinner Paolo asked her to join him in the garden and when she had seen Gino into bed, she went out there to find him. It was a bright golden evening with the sea below the garden a deep, deep blue and as calm as a mill pond. It was so clear too that she could have sworn she could see the curve of the Sorrento peninsula in the distance.

The longer shadows of evening gave the sheltered garden a soft cool look that was enchanting, and Storm suggested that they sat beside the pool on one of those ornamental white seats.

'You look very beautiful, *cara mia*!' Storm knew that the pale-blue dress she wore suited her well, and she put a tentative hand to her tawny hair and smiled. He took her hand in his, looking down at it as he lifted her fingers one by one.

'It's so much easier to *feel* beautiful here,' she told him, but did not attempt to explain her meaning.

He still did not look at her, nor did he smile, and she frowned at his bowed head curiously. She was reminded of Signora Veronese's smugness earlier, and a niggling suspicion began to rise as to the reason for both that and Paolo's reticence.

'You must look very beautiful and very—sexy— in your pretty pink *roba, carissima*.' He spoke softly, meaningly, and Storm's suspicions were confirmed, although she said nothing. His dark eyes looked up at last, deep and soulful-looking, like Gino's. 'Ah, *cara mia*, why Alexei? Why not me?' She met his eyes for a moment, not wanting to believe what was in his mind, although his words made it plain enough. 'You—you surely don't believed I asked——' She shook her head vehemently. 'You're wrong, Paolo, you're quite wrong!'

'Am I?' She did not really expect him to believe her and it was fairly obvious from his expression that he did not.

'Alexei—Signor Romano came to my room only to open a window for me. I'd closed it earlier and it was jammed, I couldn't move it.'

'I would have done it for you, *cara*.'

She shook her head. 'No, you don't understand, Paolo. I——'

'Why did you not ask me, *carissima*?' He kissed her fingers softly, his eyes dark and soulful.

Storm took a deep breath, determined to put things right. 'Paolo, will you listen to me? Please? Alexei simply came and opened a window for me, there's absolutely nothing to make a fuss about.'

'Storm! *Bellissima!*' He kissed her fingers again, shaking his head slowly. 'At one o'clock in the morning? But you do not have to explain to me, *cara*, I am not asking for excuses, you do not have to make them to me. But to ask Alexei to your room instead of me——' He put one hand on his heart and sighed. 'That is what hurts, *carissima*!'

'Paolo! Will you stop it? You're wrong, I tell you, you're quite wrong! Now please stop making such—such accusations!'

She wanted to convince him, as much for Alexei's sake as her own, she realised, but no amount of persuasion would convince Paolo. It was plain on his good-looking face that he had made up his mind, probably with the encouragement of his mother, that she had invited Alexei to her room last night for something much more serious than opening a window.

'I know you find Alexei attractive.' He took her hands again and held them in his own. 'It is that stern, cruel look, *si*? I told you that the ladies find it attractive, did I not? But he is not for you, *bellissima.* He is not a woman's man, he will not make you happy, as I will. I could not believe it when Mama said she saw him leaving your room this morning! And yet I know she would not lie to me, not even to part me from you, *cara mia!*'

And that was exactly what the Signora had hoped to achieve, Storm thought bitterly. She had hoped to turn Paolo against her so that he would give his attention to someone more eligible, but Paolo had merely expressed disappointment and was now seeking to persuade her to invite him to her room instead of his cousin. Had it not been so serious it would have been laughable, and she supposed she should have been flattered by the turn of events, but instead she felt rather as if she was getting out of her depth.

'Signora Veronese misjudged whatever it was she saw, Paolo,' she insisted. 'Gino had a nightmare and I went in to him. His cries disturbed Alexei as well and he came in to see that Gino was all right. Then I mentioned that I was so hot because the window in my room had jammed and he came in to open it for me. It's as simple as that!'

'And he was kissing you goodnight?' Paolo suggested softly, and Storm bit on her lower lip. Apparently the Signora had left out nothing.

'He—he kissed me,' she admitted reluctantly. 'I don't know why exactly. He took me by surprise and—well, he just kissed me, that's all!'

'You do not know why? He is a man, *bellissima,* and he means to have you for himself! That is not by any means all, *cara mia*!'

'Paolo!'

'Well, he shall not have you, you are mine!'

'Stop it!' She pulled her hands away from the tight clasp of his fingers and looked at him with bright, angry eyes, her breathing short and erratic as she sought for words to convince him. 'I'm *not* yours, Paolo!'

'So!' Expressive shoulders shrugged reluctant resignation. 'I have lost you to Alexei.'

'No, you haven't!'

He seemed not to hear her, however, but was intent on bemoaning his plight. 'I had never thought Alexei would take a mistress,' he said, his dark eyes reproachful and a sulky look about his mouth. 'And now he has to take *you* of all women! *Madre di Dio!* There is no justice in this world!'

'Paolo! Will you stop it!' She clenched her hands, getting to her feet, her eyes hinting at desperation. 'I have no intention of becoming Alexei's —you have no right to even suggest it!'

'But, *cara*,' Paolo told her, his eyes sad and regretful, 'he will not marry you. He is the last of the Romanos, it would not do.'

'Ooh!' Too angry and frustrated for words, Storm turned swiftly and ran into the house, leaving him staring after her, uncomprehendingly.

She started almost guiltily when she found Signora Veronese alone in the big drawing-room and stopped in her headlong flight, breathing shortly, her cheeks flushed with anger and exertion. For a moment she stood there in the open french door-way and looked at the grim-faced woman, noticing the gleam of satisfaction in her black eyes.

It was obvious that she was drawing her own conclusions about Storm's hasty departure from the garden, and the company of her son, and was well satisfied. Storm, however, was not prepared to let her have it all her own way without making some attempt to put matters right. She had been ma-ligned, her reputation torn to shreds by this woman and she meant her to know how wrong she had been.

Her heart was pit-patting nervously and she wondered how kindly Alexei Romano would take to a member of his family being put in her place, even if it was as much in his defence as her own. 'Signora Veronese.' She swallowed hard, meeting those unfriendly black eyes head on was not easy. 'You—you made a mistake last night—this morn-ing. About seeing Signor Romano—I mean——'

'I saw Signor Romano with my own eyes, *signor-ina*, leaving your room at one o'clock this morn-ing.' Her English was excellent, but Storm had never before heard her use it for so long, and her manner was cold, calm and implacable.

'And you told Paolo!'

'Of course! I was honour bound to inform my son that the woman he had been so generously entertaining was receiving her employer in her bedroom.'

'No!' Storm's green eyes blazed furiously. 'That

isn't true, *signora*, and you have no right to say it!'

The tall, gaunt figure drew itself up to full height and the autocratic Romano features condemned her out of hand. 'I saw for myself, *signorina*! I will not be called untruthful by a servant!'

'But you're wrong!'

A long hand dismissed her protestations scornfully. 'I do not care if my nephew takes a dozen mistresses, but I will not have my son involved with such a woman, *signorina*! He now sees you for what you really are, and I trust he will be rid of his foolishness and seek a suitable match in his own station of life!'

Such arrogance, Storm thought wildly, her brain spinning with anger and confusion. Such arrogance from a woman whose own son admitted that they lived on the generosity of the nephew she appeared to hold in such contempt was almost unbelievable. For a moment she said nothing, but stood with her hands clenched tightly at her sides, her eyes sparkling and angrily green.

'You may believe what you like, *signora*,' she said at last, in a voice that sounded surprisingly calm in the circumstances. 'But you are wrong in what you believe, and if you speak to Signor Romano himself about it, he will tell you so.'

One dark brow rose, and the tight lips curled derisively. 'You think I would be so indelicate, *signorina*? You are mistaken!'

It was useless, Storm realised when she looked at the hard, unrelenting features and the malicious gleam in the black eyes. No amount of talking would convince Signora Veronese, any more than it would her son and, after a moment, she shook her head and turned away, walking across the room with her back stiff and resentful, her head held high.

The double doors opened seconds before she got there and the Contessa came in, smiling when she saw her. Then the flushed cheeks and bright, angry eyes registered and she impulsively put out a hand to her. 'Storm, *cara*!' The friendly dark eyes switched quickly from Storm to the *signora* and back again. '*Cara,* what has happened?'

It was more difficult, in the face of the Contessa's obvious friendliness, to remain calm, and Storm felt a choking sensation in her throat as she shook her head. 'Oh, nothing really, Contessa, it's—it's all right.'

'*Piccola!*' Gentle hands squeezed hers sympathetically. 'It is not all right when you look so distressed, as if you would cry. Tell me what is troubling you!'

From the look she sent across the room to Signora Veronese it was obvious that she knew where the blame lay for whatever it was, and Storm was very tempted to tell her about the conclusions that Paolo and his mother had drawn from Alexei's visit to her room. Only she was afraid she would cry if she went into too much detail at the moment, so she merely shook her head, and raised the ghost of a smile.

116

'It seems to be the popular conception, Contessa, that I am Alexei's mistress!' With that she turned and ran up the stairs to her room.

Storm decided that breakfast was one meal she could afford to miss, so the following morning she did not go down as usual, but spent the time with Gino in his room, and then went straight to the makeshift schoolroom. That way she could at least avoid seeing anyone but Gino until lunch-time.

It was shortly before lunch, however, when the door opened, and she looked round with a blink of surprise. It was unusual for anyone to visit them, for Alexei had given instructions that they were not to be disturbed, and no one would dream of defying him, except possibly the Contessa, who had done so on a couple of occasions.

It was not the Contessa, however, but Alexei himself, and Storm's heart fluttered uneasily when she saw the dark, brooding look on those intriguing features. Even Gino seemed to sense that this was no time to give his uncle his usual exuberant welcome, and he merely smiled at him curiously and stayed on his chair.

'Miss Gavin, will you come to the study, please?'

He gave no preliminary greeting, and hardly even seemed to notice Gino, which was unusual. Storm nodded, glancing at her watch as she slowly closed the book she had been reading and put it down on the table, her heart rapping anxiously at her ribs.

So this was it, she thought breathlessly. This was the moment when he told her he could no longer keep her in his household. When he got rid of her as quickly as possible to prove to his aunt how wrong she was. It would have been the Contessa who told him, of course, although not with the intention of seeing her dismissed, she knew.

She managed a smile for Gino, and gave him a book of his own to look through while she was gone. 'I don't expect I'll be very long,' she told him, and wondered for the first time how Gino was going to take her going away. He had become very fond of her lately.

She followed Alexei across the few feet of gallery that separated the two rooms, her hands tightly curled into themselves. Her heart was as heavy as lead and there was a slight sensation of sickness in her stomach as she followed him into the study.

He had apparently been in the study for some time and was without his jacket, for the big room was very warm. A pale-blue shirt was open at the neck and showed a deep vee of bronze-coloured throat, with that intriguing little throb of pulse at its base. The cool colour of the shirt lent an even more icy look to his eyes and she could feel her heart racing wildly when he touched her arm and indicated a chair behind her.

He sat himself on the edge of the desk, one foot swinging slowly, light grey trousers fitting smoothly over long muscular legs. One hand clasped the opposite wrist and rested on a knee and the blue eyes regarded her steadily. It was a disconcerting experience that kept her own gaze downcast to the hands in her lap.

He was much too close for comfort and she could sense, as always, the indefinable feeling of excitement that he could always arouse in her, despite knowing what he was going to do and say.

He said nothing for several nerve-racking seconds, but took a cigarette and lit it, the smoke rising to conceal the hard, sculptured lines of those high cheekbones and the tight, straight mouth. The mouth that two nights ago had kissed her with exactly the ruthlessness it showed now.

'I have to commend you on the way you seem able to deal with Gino when he has those—bad dreams.'

It was not what she had expected to hear, and she looked at him warily, wondering if he was already unconsciously framing the words of a testimonial for her next employer.

'It only requires a little—gentleness to console a frightened child, *signore*,' she said softly, feeling a sudden and almost irresistible urge to cry.

'But you have such—gentleness.' One large hand lent meaning to the word. 'Not everyone has that gift of comforting a child.'

'Thank you.' His delaying the moment gave her the strangest feeling, as if they were antagonists, circling one another, sounding each other out, and she wanted to shout at him to please dismiss her and get it over with.

'You can see now why I did not want to send him to school until it was absolutely necessary?'

'Perhaps.' She was not really thinking about Gino, but was anxious to hear her own future decided.

It was difficult to know exactly what went on behind that carved bronze mask of a face as he studied the fingers of one hand before speaking again. 'You do not agree with me?'

She brought herself back to the subject in hand. 'No, not entirely, Signor Romano.'

The inevitable frown greeted even such an offhand admission, for he did not like criticism, as she should have remembered, and a dark brow flicked upward in question. 'You have something more to say on the matter?'

Storm hesitated, then shook her head. 'Not at this point, *signore*.' She refused to be drawn further on the matter because she felt sure he was merely delaying the moment when he had to tell her the worst.

'I see.' He got up from the desk and walked restlessly across the room, pausing only briefly by the open window, then walking back again to stand looking down at her. 'But you do not agree with the way I am dealing with Gino, *si, signorina*?'

It was so seldom that he sprinkled his English conversation with Italian words, as Paolo did, that she guessed he was more disturbed than he appeared on the surface. 'I didn't say that,' she denied quietly.

'But?' The probe was relentless, and she drew a deep breath, determined not to be drawn further.

'I—I don't want to say any more about my opinions, Signor Romano, please don't ask me.'

He looked down at her steadily, holding her gaze, despite her longing to look away, and her hands, her whole body seemed to be trembling with some wild, uncontrollable emotion that was suddenly and sharply increased when he took a step nearer suddenly. Tall, almost menacing, he stood over her and much too close for comfort.

'You are stubborn too,' he said, soft-voiced, and Storm bit her lower lip anxiously.

It was unfair of him to wreak such havoc on her senses when he knew quite well what he had to do. 'I'm sorry if you think so, *signore*.' She was appalled at the way her voice shook, and wondered if he really knew what effect he was having on her.

He turned suddenly and walked back to the window, his broad shoulders and arrogant head silhouetted against the clear blue sky, and Storm, freed of that disconcerting gaze for a few seconds, studied him surreptitiously.

It was incredible the irresistible, almost sensual feeling of intimacy he aroused when he was near her, that blood-tingling sense of excitement that persisted no matter how she tried to quell it. She had lived in his house now for well over a month and she was still not immune to it.

He turned again, and for a moment their eyes met, then he moved back across the room and stood looking down at her again, for several heart-stopping seconds. 'It was not to talk about Gino that I asked you to come here, Miss Gavin.'

'I know,' she said, and her own quietness surprised her. She looked at him for a moment then hastily down again at the hands in her lap. 'I guessed there was something else on your mind.'

'Am I so easy to read?' The deep voice was curiously gentle.

'No, not really, but it—it isn't difficult to guess what's on your mind, *signore*.'

He said nothing for a moment, but looked down at her steadily, then sat himself on the edge of the desk again. 'Of course you can guess,' he said quietly. 'I believe that my aunt has been——' Broad shoulders gave meaning to the rest of the sentence. 'For that I am sorry. I am afraid that I did rather more harm to your reputation than I realised, Miss Gavin.'

'Oh, please don't——' She knew what was going to happen next, and her heart was a tight, cold little ball inside her as she sat there waiting to hear him say it. That he was sorry about her being compromised, but he was the last of a proud old family and he could not afford to have such gossip spread about him, etc. It was inevitable, she knew, and she faced the prospect bleakly.

'Unfortunately the incidence of my being in a woman's room at that hour of the night is sufficiently novel for it to have aroused more comment than if I had been——' He did not complete the sentence, but it was obvious to anyone that he referred to Paolo.

Storm sat still, for a moment, her head bowed, looking at the folded hands on her lap and feeling as if all the world had suddenly come to a standstill. The tawny thickness of her hair swung forward and hid her face, and she looked very small and rather defenceless sitting there on the ornate gilt chair in that big sunny room.

'You'd like me to leave, Signor Romano.' It was a statement, not a question, for she told herself there could be no other answer. 'Of course, I understand.'

'Leave?'

She looked up hastily, something in his voice setting a new hope skipping through her heart, and she found the ice-blue eyes watching her steadily and with a small frown between his brows. 'I—I thought——' The words refused to come, and instead she shook her head slowly, wondering what possible alternative he could offer.

'It was at my instigation that I came to your room, Miss Gavin.' He sounded more businesslike suddenly, as if he had made up his mind about something and would not be persuaded otherwise. 'You pointed out to me yourself, at the time, that you did not invite me, and therefore the onus is upon me to take the right steps to remedy the harm I have done.'

'I—I don't understand.' She got to her feet, for it was difficult to talk to him in this vein while she was sitting down, and so much out of touch with him.

'Since you said as much to the Contessa, you are fully aware that Paolo and my aunt have decided that you are my mistress, and since my aunt is not a woman to keep such gossip to herself, by tomorrow when she has visited her dressmaker again, half of Naples will know it.'

Put so bluntly it sounded crude and far worse than she had feared and she felt the blood pounding wildly against her temple as she clenched her hands. 'But it's—it's ridiculous! You know it isn't true and so do I!'

'Have you tried to convince Paolo?' he asked softly, and Storm nodded, her eyes dark and unhappy.

'He didn't believe me.'

'Of course not! Paolo, unfortunately, attributes more of the family traits to me than he should. He imagines that my mind travels along the same devious routes as his own.'

The blue eyes had an icy look again, and she could imagine something of the beating his pride had taken at the hands of his cousin and his aunt. The accusation was not true, but the only evidence was that of Signora Veronese's malicious eyes and she would never consider giving him the benefit of the doubt, especially if she thought it would convince her son of Storm's promiscuity.

She could even imagine that Paolo would find it to his liking, in one way, to have his autocratic cousin at his mercy, trying to explain what he was doing in her room in the early hours of the morning. Paolo was charming and attractive, but he had been prepared to believe that she had invited Alexei to her room for one reason only, and had even expressed his jealousy.

'I—I don't know what to say, Signor Romano.' She looked up at the dark, chiselled features appealingly, feeling completely at a loss. If he did not expect her to leave, what possible alternative could there be?

'It was unfortunate, to say the least, but you were completely blameless and in the circumstances I was forced to act as I thought best.' He spoke in a cool, quiet voice while Storm looked at him from under her lashes, her heart uneasily tapping at her ribs as she waited. 'There was very little point in denying that I was in your room at all and, since family history is very much against my visit being as innocent as it was, I have taken the only step possible.'

'You—you have?'

She eyed him warily, green eyes anxious, one hand nervously pushing the tawny hair from her face, and he did not look at her when he spoke, but ground out the remains of the cigarette in an ashtray, with fingers that showed white with the force he used. 'I said that I intended to marry you and it was therefore quite in order for me to visit you, briefly, in the privacy of your bedroom.'

Storm held her breath, refusing to believe she

had heard him aright. Her heart was hammering so loudly that she felt sure it must be audible to him as he stood there, tall and so dismayingly composed, reaching for another cigarette and lighting it.

'You—you seriously mean to tell me that you——'

'I am not likely to jest about such a serious matter, Miss Gavin—Storm.' He added her Christian name, as if it was part of his new role to use it and he meant to play it well.

'But you don't have to marry me,' she whispered, a hand to her throat where a pulse throbbed uncontrollably.

'You expected me to dismiss you out of hand?' he demanded, and she realised for the first time how she had wronged him by thinking just that.

'I'm—I'm sorry. But you don't have to go that far to make things right for me, Signor Romano. It—it doesn't make sense!'

The arrogant bronze features, like some ancient carving, with ice-blue eyes glittering above those high, Slav cheekbones, looked stern and harsh and she could feel the tension that held his temper in check. It struck her like a blow and she put her hands to her mouth as if to make sure no other words escaped.

'Do I understand that you find the idea of marriage to me so distasteful that you reject it out of hand?' She could have curled up and died at the scorn he put into his voice, and almost instinctively she shook her head.

'No, no, of course not, but——'

'Or perhaps you preferred being thought of as my mistress!'

'Oh, please, I——'

Storm was horrified to discover that there were tears in her eyes and she hastily brushed them away with a trembling hand. Before she could recover herself completely, however, strong brown fingers reached out and touched her cheek gently, and again that familiar sensation of excitement swept through her at his touch.

'I have perhaps been too abrupt in telling you as I have,' he said softly, and in such contrast to his earlier harshness that she scarcely believed it possible. 'I have not, as you will have already discovered, Paolo's gift for acting the courtier.'

Storm looked up at him hazily, unsure whether to respond to this more gentle mood, or to be on her guard in case he changed back again as quickly. 'What did Paolo say to—to——'

'To the idea of my marrying you?' For a brief moment the wide, straight mouth tilted into a half smile. 'I believe that he was too stunned at the time to say very much at all, but I have no doubt that he will remedy that when he has had time to get used to the idea.' The blue eyes regarded her for a moment steadily. 'And you—what have you to say, Storm?'

She turned and walked over to the window, looking down at the garden below, at the tall trees and the pool glinting in the bright July sunshine and making little dappled patterns on the ceiling. He must, she thought, have taken advantage of her absence from breakfast to make his pronouncement and she thanked heaven that she had stayed with Gino instead of going down as she usually did.

It required a lot of thinking about, the idea of marrying Alexei, in the prevailing circumstances, but she doubted if she would be given very much time. Alexei Romano was a man who made up his mind and acted without hesitation, expecting everyone else to do the same.

'I—I can't think straight at the moment,' she said without turning to look at him.

'You find it very difficult to accept?'

Storm shook her head hastily. 'Oh no, not—not really.' She turned then and looked over her shoulder at him. 'I've talked to the Contessa,' she said softly, and the blue eyes showed understanding. 'She said——' She hesitated to go on, to be too frank with the Contessa's confidences, but he was watching her and she found the blue-eyed gaze very hard to resist. 'She said you would have married Gino's mother if you had been in—in your brother's place.'

For a brief second he frowned, as if he resented the criticism of his dead brother, and she feared she had gone too far, but then he shrugged, and the frown vanished. 'Perhaps I would have done,' he admitted, but Storm felt in her heart that he quite definitely would have done. If he was prepared to do so much for her, how much more would he have

128

been prepared to do for the mother of his child?

'She is a wonderful woman, the Contessa,' she ventured, and he nodded firm agreement this time.

'As I know better than most,' he said. 'And knowing about the Contessa you will better understand my decision now. It is an invidious position for any woman, and I have vowed that no woman shall ever find herself in such a position because of any action of mine.'

'I'm grateful for your consideration, Signor Romano.'

'I do not know how grateful you should be,' he told her. 'That remains to be seen, it will of course make no difference to you, except that you will now have the protection of being my fiancée and later my wife——'

'But surely,' Storm interrupted swiftly, 'if we—if you become merely engaged to me it will be enough to—to solve the problem.'

Again the blue eyes looked at her icily and the firm mouth tightened ominously. 'You seem determined to avoid marrying me,' he said brusquely. 'I find your reluctance rather odd in the circumstances, *signorina*, and not very flattering!'

'Oh, but I didn't mean——' She gazed at him with dismay. 'I didn't mean to sound either evasive or—or unflattering,' she said. 'I'm sorry, it's just that—I don't want you to go through with anything you'll regret later, Signor Romano.'

He made no move to join her by the window and she thanked heaven for it, for he disturbed her as no man had ever done before, and she needed time to think. 'I do not anticipate having any regrets,' he said quietly. 'And I think it would be as well if you called me Alexei. Such formality from my future wife might fall oddly on other ears.'

She was too shy to experiment with it at the moment, but moved across and stood beside him again. 'Of course.'

'Perhaps you think I am too concerned with matters that many people take for granted now,' he suggested, and Storm shook her head.

'No, no, of course I don't.'

He sat on the edge of the desk and she could see his strong brown hands gripping the polished wood, feeling an inexplicable urge to reach out and touch them. 'My father, my brother—for generations the Romanos have taken what women they wanted and thought it their right.' He sounded so harsh in his judgment that Storm felt a small cold shiver of apprehension trickle down her spine for a moment, then he looked up and held her gaze. 'So you see there was plenty of foundation for Aunt Sofia's suspicions.'

He straightened up suddenly, standing over her tall and straight, his unusual features showing a strange hint of anxiety as he watched her face. 'Now, Storm, will you give me your answer?'

Faced with an immediate decision, when she had thought the matter cut and dried, she almost panicked. Her heart was thudding wildly at her ribs and she felt her legs so weak and trembling that she feared they might at any moment let her down.

Then she looked at the dark, strongly defined features and the ice-blue eyes below dark brows, and knew what she would say even before the words formed on her lips. 'I will marry you, Alexei,' she said in a huskily soft voice.

CHAPTER SEVEN

IT was three weeks since they were married, a quiet ceremony in Naples, with the warm September sun lending a rather inappropriate air of sadness to the occasion. Storm was not yet used to being addressed as Signora Romano, but it gave her a strange feeling of panic each time she heard it, wondering if she had made a mistake in taking such an irrevocable step.

Not that her life had changed very much in any other way, for Alexei seemed to consider he had done as much as was required of him when he gave her his name. She still occupied her own room, with Gino's room between her and Alexei, an arrangement that Signora Veronese had viewed with much raising of brows and pursing of her thin lips.

It was obvious that the Contessa thought it a disgraceful state of affairs, and Storm suspected that she had said as much, quite bluntly, to Alexei. Paolo, on the other hand, took it as a good sign for his own future activities, and had once or twice tried to tempt Storm to go out with him for an evening.

She had resisted his attempts so far, but the weather was so lovely and there was so much that she had not seen yet that she thought she would be bound to succumb before very long, if he persisted. Being Paolo, of course, he persisted, and at last she weakened.

It was a lovely day, the sun warm enough to be comfortable and without the sultry heat of summer, and Paolo had put his head round the door, smiling hopefully. It was only mid-morning and Storm glanced at her watch, frowning at him curiously and demanding to know what he was doing there instead of being at the works.

'I am—how is it?—playing truant,' he told her with an irresistible smile, and Gino laughed, sharing his secret willingly.

'But, Paolo, if you——'

'*Quièto.*' He put a finger over her lips and silenced her, then turned to Gino with a sly wink. '*Vade via*, Gino, hah?'

Gino beamed knowingly, put down his book and went out on to the balcony while Paolo took his seat beside Storm. She tried not to smile, but Paolo reminded her so much of Gino and his mischief that she was hard put to keep a straight face as he took her hands in his and leaned towards her, his smile persuasive.

'Paolo——'

'Ssh!' Again that silencing finger lay across her mouth. 'Where shall we go, *cara mia*?'

'Paolo, I can't go anywhere with you, you know that. I have to give Gino his lessons.'

'Lessons, pah!' He dismissed the idea scornfully. 'Does the Signora Romano give lessons like a *governante*? You are Signora Romano, *bellissima mia*!

You should remember that!'

'I was wondering if *you* remembered it,' Storm told him quietly. 'It isn't quite the same now, Paolo, is it?'

'Ah, Storm, *bella mia*! I have taken this chance to be with you, are you cruel enough to dismiss me? It is only for a little time, *carissima*, a little ride, hmm?'

It was inevitable, Storm recognised as she met those persuasive dark eyes, that she would surrender, but she did so with some misgivings. 'All right,' she said with a sigh. 'I'll come with you, Paolo, but only for a while.'

'*Bene*! Where shall we go, *cara mia*?'

She shook her head, laughing despite herself at his pleasure in persuading her at last. 'There are so many places I'd like to see,' she told him. 'For instance, I'd like to go to Pompeii. It isn't very far away, is it?'

'Pompeii?' He looked appalled at her choice, his dismayed expression making her laugh again. Paolo always made her laugh, he was very good for her morale, and truth to tell Alexei took very little more notice of her than he had before, and she found it somehow demoralising.

'I'd like to see Pompeii,' she insisted. 'But if you don't want to take me, I can go alone and get myself a guide.'

'And get yourself a lot of trouble from Alexei also, *cara mia*!' He rolled his eyes expressively. 'Do you think he would allow you to go walking around with a guide, like a tourist, and alone? *Madre di Dio!*'

'Well, he never takes me anywhere himself, so I haven't much choice, have I?' She wished, as soon as the words had left her lips, that she had not said that, and Paolo's smile confirmed the rashness of it.

He leaned across and kissed her on her mouth, the first time he had even attempted to do so since her marriage, and his dark eyes glowed warmly. 'Oh, *povera piccola*! I will take pity on you, *si*?'

He seemed not to care that Gino was no further away than a chair on the balcony, and that they were quite audible to him. She dared not think, either, what Alexei would say if he knew he was there, and she wondered, yet again, why he *was* there.

'Paolo, how have you managed to come back here?' she asked. 'Does Alexei know you're playing truant?'

He shrugged, very casual and offhand. 'Maybe— I am supposed to be fetching some plans from the study. It was a good excuse to see you, *carissima*!'

Again he leaned across and kissed her mouth and she drew back, glancing out on to the balcony and Gino apparently engrossed in the vista below the window. 'Paolo, please don't do that!' She had to chance that Gino would tell his uncle about this surreptitious visit, and she sincerely hoped he would not.

'Oh, *cara*!' His mouth sought hers again, but this time she managed to evade him, pushing at him with both hands when he attempted to get even closer. He looked down at her soft mouth and sighed deeply. 'He does not kiss you either, does he?' he asked softly. 'Such a pity, *cara mia*! If I had such a beautiful wife I would not spend all my time at the works!'

'If you had a wife I doubt if you'd spend much time with *her* either!' Storm retorted, and laughed when he looked at her reproachfully. 'You're not the marrying kind, Paolo.'

'Nor is Alexei, it seems,' Paolo retaliated. 'He has not made a very good husband so far, *carissima*, has he?'

Storm frowned, looking down at her hands and shaking her head. 'Please don't say things like that, Paolo,' she said. 'There are things you don't understand, and Alexei *is* my husband, I don't like to hear him maligned.'

'Then he should behave like a husband!' He took her hands in his and kissed the fingertips gently, his dark eyes persuasive. 'But at least his not caring allows me to take you out, *bella mia, si*?' He shrugged resignedly and pulled a face. 'If you want to go to Pompeii, then that is where we will go, but not with Gino, huh?'

Storm glanced again at the little figure on the balcony, his black head turned away from them but probably fully aware of all that was going on. 'I can't leave him, Paolo,' she said, and he frowned impatiently.

'But of course you can, *cara*. Lisetta will take

care of him for a few hours—if I ask her to!' He rolled his dark eyes wickedly, and Storm had no doubt that Lisetta would do as he asked, but whether Signora Veronese would be so co-operative was another matter. If anyone told Alexei about their outing it would be his aunt.

'I don't know.'

'Oh, *cara mia!*' He leaned forward and kissed her unexpectedly, so that she had no time to draw back. 'You get ready and I will go and beg Lisetta to be *bambinaia* for a little while, *si?*'

Storm sighed resignedly. Arguing with Paolo was almost as useless as arguing with Alexei about anything. It got one nowhere. '*Si,*' she echoed, and he kissed her again lightly as he got to his feet.

Storm watched him go, already having second thoughts about the wisdom of going, especially as Paolo was taking absence without leave from the works. Then she sighed and went out to explain to Gino.

He was curled up on the seat and he turned and looked at her with that mischievous, knowing look. 'Zio Paolo is very—ya, ya, ya!' His eyes rolled wickedly and Storm shook her head at him.

'Gino, please don't talk like that! Your Uncle Paolo and I are simply——' She shrugged, acknowledging the futility of trying to explain. Explanations would probably involve her even more deeply than she was already, and she sighed again, resignedly. 'You won't mind staying with Zia Lisetta for a while, will you darling, while I go out for a drive?'

'With Zio Paolo?' He reached up and put his hand in hers. 'Where are you going, Zia Tempesta?' He had been told to address her as aunt, but the Italian version sounded so much prettier that she had encouraged him to use that instead.

'We're going to Pompeii. Have you ever been there?'

She half hoped he would ask to come too, for she would have been happier with Gino along, despite Paolo's dislike of the idea, but Gino shrugged his shoulders with Latin disregard for history. 'It is only old stones,' he told her scornfully. 'The tourist goes there. I do not want to go.'

She smiled at his scorn and bent to kiss the top of his head lightly. 'Then you will not mind staying with Zia Lisetta while I go, will you?'

He shook his head, his huge dark eyes looking up at her as wisely as an old man. 'And I will not tell Zio Alexei where you have gone,' he promised gravely.

'Gino!' She looked at him appalled at the suggestion of intrigue, but Gino seemed quite unperturbed.

'You go,' he urged her solemnly, but with a belying glint in his eyes. 'I do not mind. You will have fun, no?'

Storm opened her mouth to protest again, but there seemed little point in the face of that mischievous look, she was defeated before she began.

Instead she bent and kissed him again on his fore-head.

'You're far too much like your Uncle Paolo,' she told him firmly. '*Ciao*, Gino!'

Storm made no secret of the fact that she enjoyed being with Paolo, and she told herself that Alexei had no real cause to complain in the circumstances. It was not as if theirs was an ordinary marriage, or that Alexei ever showed any inclination to take her out anywhere. He was not a man who enjoyed the social life, but preferred to give all his time and energy to the affairs of the companies he ran.

Paolo, on the other hand, gave only as much time as he was obliged to to the companies, and as much time as possible to enjoying himself. In the circumstances, Storm felt, Alexei was very lenient with him.

He obviously would have preferred to drive to one of the charming little resorts along the coast and swim, or just laze on the beach, but Storm had insisted on going to Pompeii, and he had yielded eventually with one of those all-embracing shrugs. She somehow felt that a trip of that sort would appear less reprehensible to Alexei than merely lazing on a beach somewhere.

The drive out to the ruined city made the jour-ney well worthwhile without any other induce-ment, and she enjoyed it immensely. It was the same motorway that passed the villa and along which they had travelled to Naples, but this time they had turned the other way and come further south, turning off when they got nearer their destination.

Paolo always drove as if there was some emergency at the other end of the journey, and this time Storm did not hesitate to ask him to drive more slowly. To give her time to appreciate the breathtaking views that the journey offered.

'It's so beautiful,' she told him. 'I want to be able to appreciate it, Paolo.'

Obligingly he reduced speed, and pulled a face at her over one shoulder. '*Si, signora!* Your word is my command! Is that not the phrase, *cara mia?*'

'It is,' Storm agreed. 'But I doubt very much if it's true in this case!'

'Oh, come, *bellissima*, have I not slowed down so much that I am almost standing still, so that you may see the countryside?'

'Don't you want to see it too?' she asked, laughing at his exaggerated claim. 'It's very lovely, and I'm sure no one ever gets blasé about such scenery.'

'It is very beautiful,' Paolo agreed with a smile. 'And so are you, *carissima*. You go together, you and this beautiful country.'

'I hope so.' Somehow his words made her feel wistful suddenly, and she looked at the wonderful country around them, wishing Alexei could have found the time to show it to her.

At times they seemed almost to be hovering on the edge of the cliffs above the deep, sparkling blue Mediterranean, with a carpet of trees and vines between. On the other side were the inevitable acres and acres of citrus groves and the many other crops that this lush, fertile land produced.

The neat compact orange trees with their waxy and fragrant blooms and golden fruits, and the untidier, more straggly lemons with their purple blossom and green fruit. The groves filled the air with their scent as well as providing a colourful picture under the paler blue sky of the dying year and Storm found it all endlessly enjoyable.

A woman, watching her man at work under the twisty grey trunks of olive trees, raised her head from the knitting that absorbed her and crinkled her weathered brown face into a toothless smile when Storm waved a hand at them. It was a refreshing, carefree ride and she felt grateful to Paolo for suggesting it, turning to smile at him and catching his eye.

'*Cara?*' He smiled enquiringly, and Storm shook her head.

'I'm just very—happy,' she told him, laughing softly. 'Why should I be anything else?'

'Why should you, *po' gugina?*'

She looked at him curiously. 'That's a new name for me,' she said. 'What does *that* one mean? Or shouldn't I ask?'

Paolo's shoulders shrugged carelessly. 'Why should you not, *cara?* It is only little cousin.'

'Oh, I see. Yes, I suppose I am your cousin now, aren't I?'

'Since Alexei married you, I suppose you are,' he

agreed. 'Although I wish he had left you free, *cara mia*, or else would make a proper wife of you. This way you are a temptation just out of reach, and yet not fully appreciated by anyone.'

'Paolo, please!'

She did not want to discuss her relationship with Alexei, especially at this moment, when she was feeling so delightfully lighthearted. The ride had brought colour to her cheeks and a bright shine to her green eyes and she looked quite beautiful, especially to Paolo's appreciative eyes.

'It is such a waste, *carissima*!'

'It's *my* concern—and Alexei's,' she told him quietly. 'Now please don't let's talk about anything, Paolo. I want to enjoy my ride.'

'And talking about Alexei would spoil it for you?'

She looked at him for a moment, at the good-looking profile and the long lashes that swept down to half conceal his eyes, making shadows on the golden brown face. He was very good-looking and very attractive and she sometimes wondered if she could fall deeply in love with him, but then there was always Alexei. Alexei had married her and behaved as if he was still her employer—Paolo behaved as a newly acquired husband could be expected to behave, but would never have married her, she felt sure. It was a confusing situation one way and another, and she sometimes wondered how it would all eventually evolve.

Pompeii, when they eventually arrived, proved

just as interesting as she had expected, and she was thankful to find it fairly free of visitors, thanks to the lateness of the time of year. There were visitors, but not the endless crowds that swarmed through the ancient city during the height of summer.

There seemed such a sense of occasion about seeing a place that had, until now, been no more than something she had read about at school. Tall fluted columns, the remnants of beautiful villas and temples, rose up into the clear sky, looking surprisingly new and giving some idea of how impressive the living city must have been.

Avenues, rediscovered from the all-enveloping dust of centuries, where wealthy families one lived, their well-worn routes now trodden by thousands of foreign feet and laid out in the all-revealing sun.

She discovered the temple of the god Apollo and was immediately attracted by the huge bronze statue of him that stood on a stone block amid the steps and fluted columns that had once been raised to his glory. It was a wonderful piece of work, with the god poised for flight, his hands extended as if they had once held the bow and golden arrow with which he slew the monster, Python.

There was such a sense of life about the statue, such perfection in its craftsmanship that she felt herself compelled to stand before it in admiration as one of those ancient worshippers might have done.

Paolo waited for her, none too patiently, leaning

against some nearby steps and not nearly as enthralled as she was by his surroundings. 'Storm!'

His voice recalled her, and she abandoned her daydream reluctantly. 'Have I been here too long?' she asked, smiling at his impatience, and he laughed softly, coming across to put an arm round her shoulders.

'You have been admiring Apollo for long enough, *cara mia*, I shall be envious if you give him any more of your time.'

'I'm sorry.'

'That I shall be envious of him?'

She shook her head, pushing back the tawny hair from her flushed face and laughing. 'No, that I kept you waiting. You've been very patient.' She glanced at the small gold watch on her wrist and frowned anxiously. 'The time's gone so quickly, I think we'd better go back, Paolo.'

'You think your *hus*band will miss you?'

He sounded very scornful of the likelihood of that being so and Storm felt her cheeks colour furiously. She did not know for certain whether or not Alexei would mind her being with Paolo, but she was quite sure he would be angry about Paolo taking leave from the works to take her out and she would have liked to be back before he returned and found them still missing. Also she did not like to hear Paolo make such obviously scathing remarks about his cousin.

'I think he probably will miss me,' she said quietly.

'As he misses any of his property that is missing for a while,' he declared, and Storm clenched her hands, her eyes sparkling angrily.

'Paolo, you have no right to talk like that!'

Paolo, however, was in no mood to be tactful and his dark, good-looking face betrayed a jealousy she had never seen before, and which startled her in its vehemence. 'I have no rights about anything,' he said harshly. 'I am the *povre cugino*—the poor relation! I have no rights, no property, no—Oh, *Madre di Dio*! Sometimes I could hate Alexei!'

'Paolo! Please don't—don't say that!' Storm put a hand on his arm and looked up at him anxiously. She had never before seen him express such resentment, and she wondered what had suddenly given rise to such passion.

For a moment he said nothing, but gazed at her in silence with those warm, dark eyes that were so like Gino's, then he moved closer and put an arm right round her waist, hugging her close to him, his lips pressed to her neck. 'I am sorry, *carissima*,' he whispered, then drew back and looked at her with a comically rueful face. 'I am anticipating what Alexei will say when I see him again,' he told her. 'I know I shall be—how is it you say?'

'For the high jump?' Storm suggested quietly, and laughed when he pulled another face.

'*Si, si!* Alexei will put me to the high jump as he does his horses, and I shall have to jump too, *bella mia*, or he will crack the whip as he does at them!'

She remembered her own first estimation of

Alexei. How she had visualised him as a crabby old man who cracked the whip and expected everyone to jump. She had been wrong in the first part of her estimation, but not, it seemed, in the second.

'Poor Paolo!'

She could do nothing about the laughter that glinted in her eyes for his outrageous self-pity, and he tightened his hold on her suddenly, pulling her round into his arms. They were in a quiet corner, away from the scattered crowd of visitors, but she was not at all happy about the situation, and put her hands to his chest to try to ward him off, for his intention was obvious.

'You are cruel,' he accused, in a softly husky voice that betrayed his intent as clearly as his actions did. 'Like all beautiful women you are cruel, *carissima*. You laugh at my fate, you find it amusing that your husband will presently——' A great sigh vibrated through her as well, and he drew her even closer, despite her attempt to stop him.

'Paolo!'

He kissed her softly and lingeringly. *'Carissima!'* he whispered, and Storm closed her eyes slowly.

It was something she should not allow, she knew that quite well, but there was something irresistible about Paolo always, and she could feel a persistent little pulse tapping away at her temple, telling her she was enjoying being kissed by Paolo again, married woman or not.

'Please don't, Paolo!'

She regained breath enough at last to push him away, but he stayed close enough to be disturbing, his arms still holding her close. 'Oh, *cara*, who is to know?' He kissed her again beside her left ear, moving aside the tawny hair, his fingers gently caressing against her skin.

'No, Paolo, please!'

She put her hands to his chest again and pushed hard against the strength of his arms, and as she turned her head to avoid another kiss she stared, her lips parted, her eyes huge with surprise. Paolo, his eyes on her face, frowned curiously at her.

'Storm? What is it?'

Then he too turned his head and a second later stepped back hastily. There was no mistaking the tall striding figure in light grey trousers and a white shirt, his hands swinging loosely at his sides as he came towards them. There was an air of menace about Alexei Romano that lent grimness to those bronzed, chiselled features and sent a shiver of apprehension through Storm's body.

Even from yards away she could see that those ice-blue eyes had never been icier, and she wondered which one of them was the target for most of his anger. Neither of them said a word, but waited for the striding figure to reach them and Storm could feel her heart thudding away heavily at her ribs.

It was the first time she had ever felt this strange, almost elated sense of anticipation, and she told herself it was fear for what would happen to Paolo, but somewhere in her brain something kept reminding her that this figure of vengeance striding towards them was her husband. It was a curiously exciting sensation to realise it so suddenly.

He came to a halt immediately in front of Paolo, ignoring Storm completely for the moment, so that she instinctively stepped back. His voice was steel-edged, and much more harsh than she had ever heard it before.

'You left to fetch some plans, I understand,' he said, and Paolo nodded. There was a faint hint of defiance in his dark eyes, but Storm doubted if it would come to maturity.

'I forgot about them,' he said, as sulkily as Gino might have done. 'I am sorry, Alexei.'

'You preferred to drive around the countryside with my wife, it seems, while Picerni waited for the plans.'

The claim to her as his wife had a chilling sound, and offered no hint of jealousy, certainly not of affection, and Storm could feel herself almost literally shrinking. She wished the dusty ground beneath her feet would swallow her up into the same volcanic oblivion as the city it had once buried.

'*Ma*, Alexei, *lei si è sbagliato*——'

'My wife does not speak Italian.' The cold voice cut across his words. 'Please speak in English.'

He meant to humiliate Paolo as much as possible in front of her, that much was obvious, and Storm's senses rebelled at the harshness of it. She stuck out her chin defiantly, well knowing that he would dislike her intervention, but determined on it just the same.

'There's no need to make quite so much fuss about it, surely,' she said in a voice that she wished could have been more firm and less liable to shake and betray her feelings. 'It was—it was my fault as much as Paolo's that we came here, and I'm sorry if you've been inconvenienced, Alexei, but please don't take it out on Paolo.'

For a second he did not move or speak, and she wondered if he was going to ignore her still, although she could feel the anger that emanated from him, and her hands were trembling as she held tightly on to her handbag. Then he turned slowly and looked down at her, his eyes as cold as ice, but at the same time blazing angrily.

'I do not need to be informed that you were in part to blame for this expedition,' he said coldly. 'But I have also no doubt whatever that Paolo was the instigator.' He looked at his cousin again, stern-faced and unrelenting, his dark head held arrogantly so that the square chin thrust aggressively. 'You will drive back to the works and take the plans to Picerni,' he told him.

Instinctively Paolo glanced at Storm, and Alexei was on to the glance in a moment. 'I will drive my wife back,' he said.

'I'd rather drive back with Paolo!'

She had no idea what on earth prompted her to say such a thing, and for a moment both men stared at her in disbelief, then Paolo shook his head slowly, his dark eyes appealing with her to change her mind.

'You will drive with me!' Alexei said, and looked at his cousin. *'Andare immediatamente, Paolo, per favore!'*

Paolo, after one last glance of resignation at Storm, turned and walked off to where they had parked the car, and she watched him go with a certain feeling of guilt. It was true that he had persuaded her to come out with him, but if she had been more adamant in her refusal this whole incident would never have happened, and she fervently wished it hadn't.

She did not look directly at Alexei, but only glanced up through her lashes, not encouraged by the grim, angry look of him still. Then, without a word, he suddenly took her arm in a grip of iron and took her along beside him as he too headed for the parking place. His long stride made it necessary for her to half run to keep pace with him, and she felt rather like a runaway child being brought back by an irate parent.

'Stop it!' She stood her ground suddenly, although he almost pulled her over as he went on. His fingers eased slightly on her arm, but he still held on to her and she knew it was useless to try and shake free. 'I—I can't keep up with you, Alexei, and I refuse to be hauled through this place like a runaway slave!'

For a moment she could have sworn that a glint of amusement showed briefly in his eyes, but then he set his mouth firmly straight and looked down at her icily. 'You have used that simile once before about our relationship,' he told her quietly. 'And I might tell you, *fanciulla mia,* that this is a time when I wish you *could* be bought and sold!'

'Oh, if you want to get rid of me,' Storm told him rashly, 'that's simple enough! You just send me packing!'

The dark, strong features did not change their expression, but something in his eyes did, and she shivered as she saw the change. He held her gaze, and she could feel the heavy thudding of her heart against her ribs, and that strange sense of elation again.

'Would you go?' he asked softly, but gave her no time to answer. He started walking again, taking her along with him, although at a much less hazardous pace. 'You are required to be Signora Romano, officially, tonight,' he told her brusquely, and for a moment Storm's heart fluttered wildly until she realised she had misunderstood him.

'How?' she asked breathlessly. 'I mean—I mean where?'

The ice-blue eyes looked down at her for a moment, a gleam of speculation in their depths so that she hastily lowered her own. 'Oh, do not fear,' he said quietly. 'I simply require you to act as hostess to an important business acquaintance.'

'Oh! Oh, I see.'

'You have a suitable gown, I know,' he went on, while Storm tried to still the sudden sense of panic that filled her at the idea. 'You will have time when we get back to change and make yourself presentable in time for his arrival, although you would have been better prepared if you had been at home when I arrived.'

'I'm sorry.'

He opened the car door and helped her in, his dark, chiselled features coming close as he bent to tuck her skirt in over her knees. 'I trust you will prove that by not doing such a thing again,' he said quietly, and Storm flushed with resentment.

'I'm sorry I inconvenienced you by not being there when you arrived home,' she told him, rashly uncaring. 'I'm not sorry I went out with Paolo. I like going out and you——' She bit on her lip hastily when she felt him slide into the driving seat alongside her, his bare arm brushing against hers, the vibrant warmth of him tingling against her skin.

He started the engine, then turned his head and looked at her steadily. 'You find me very much lacking as a husband,' he suggested, and she did not answer. 'I imagined that you had your needs in that direction well taken care of by Paolo. You do not need anything from me, *amante*.'

Storm would have argued, would have told him he was wrong about her feeling for Paolo, only he would have seen her being kissed in the ruins of Apollo's temple, and drawn his own conclusions. She must, she thought as an afterthought, ask Paolo what *amante* meant.

CHAPTER EIGHT

PAOLO did not return to the villa until some time after Storm and Alexei got back. Storm was leaving her bathroom, half dressed, and on her way back to her bedroom when she saw him, and chanced Alexei making a sudden appearance to ask about the visitor they were expecting. Apart from saying that he was coming, Alexei had been annoyingly uncommunicative about him.

'Sir Gerald Gordon,' Paolo informed her. 'Very wealthy and very English, *carissima*.'

'English?' She looked surprised at that. 'Alexei didn't tell me he was English.'

'Perhaps he was hoping to surprise you.' Paolo's dark eyes swept over her slim figure covered by a pale blue robe that was flimsy enough to reveal the contours under it without it being transparent. 'You look very beautiful, *carissima*. That robe is— Mmm!' He kissed his fingertips extravagantly, and Storm shook her head, glancing along at Alexei's door as she spoke.

'I'd better go and dress,' she said. 'Before Alexei comes looking for me.'

Paolo's dark eyes glowed wickedly. 'If he sees you in that *roba, bella mia*, you will melt even his icy Russian heart. *Madre di Dio*, but he is no Romano, that one!'

'Paolo, please!'

'But he does not appreciate you, *bellissima*, and therefore he does not deserve you!'

'Please don't——'

A faint sound from further along the gallery made them both glance towards Alexei's bedroom door, but before his cousin appeared Paolo had slipped swiftly in the bathroom that Storm had just vacated. Storm had some vain hope of hurrying along to her own room and slipping in without being seen while Alexei was closing his door, but it was a very vain hope in the circumstances.

It was not customary for them to dress formally for dinner, but tonight was a special occasion, and it was the first time Storm had seen Alexei in a dinner jacket. The expensively tailored white mohair jacket fitted his lean frame perfectly and each movement he made revealed the smooth ripple of muscle in his arms and shoulders.

There was a hint of frilled shirt cuff showing at each wrist, saved from effeminacy by the strong brown hands, and the whiteness of the shirt and jacket gave his dark head and bronzed features an almost primitive arrogance that set the blood tinging in her veins at the sight of him. And for the second time that day she reminded herself that this man was her husband.

It was evident from the way he looked at her that he appreciated the flimsy revelation of the blue robe, although whether it melted his icy Russian heart, as Paolo had said it would, was debatable.

The blue eyes made a swift, calculated appraisal of her from head to foot, and then regarded her steadily for a moment. There was still a hint of that cold anger she had seen on their earlier encounter, but the worst of it had vanished, apparently, and she thanked heaven for it.

'You will have to hurry if you are to be ready in good time!'

Storm looked at him, feeling a little guilty, especially when she thought of Paolo disappearing into her bathroom, and she fervently hoped Alexei had not seen him go in. She nodded, but did not venture to smile. 'I know I have to hurry.' She hesitated, and her hesitation sent a dark brow upwards in query. 'Alexei, I—I wondered if you'd mind my not wearing the green dress after all.'

He had especially asked her to wear a particular gown, mostly, she suspected, because it was very grand and luxurious. It was a beautiful and very expensive gown of deep jade green slipper satin and it gave her a feeling of almost sensual pleasure to feel its smooth shiny folds around her. The problem was that it had a zip fastener the whole lenth of its back seam. It would be hopeless for her to try and struggle with it herself, and the one and only maid allocated to such duties was already busy with Signora Veronese and the Contessa, and likely to be for some time yet.

'May I ask why you do not want to wear it?' he asked.

'It isn't that I don't want to wear it,' Storm explained, hoping this wasn't a prelude to an argument. 'But Clemente is busy with Signora Veronese and the Contessa, and I can't reach the zip at the back of the green dress to fasten it myself. I thought that if I wore——'

'I prefer that you wear the green one!'

So, Storm thought, he was going to be stubborn about it, and she looked at him reproachfully, disappointed that he would not unbend sufficiently to be reasonable. 'Then you'll have to forgive me if I'm late,' she told him. 'I'll have to wait for Clemente to come and help me.'

'There is no need—I will help you.'

She stared at him for a moment unbelievingly, her pulses racing furiously at the prospect of having him do anything as personal and intimate as helping her to dress. 'You—you will?'

A small frown of impatience drew his dark brows together. 'I *am* your husband,' he reminded her shortly.

'Oh yes, yes, of course!'

'You find it easy to forget that, hmm?'

Storm sighed inwardly, guessing that she would not be allowed to forget that visit to Pompeii in a hurry. Alexei would make sure of that. 'No, I don't find it easy at all,' she denied quietly, determined not to be provoked. 'And if I'm to be ready in time, I *must* go and finish dressing. If you'll excuse me.'

'I have said I will help you with your gown.'

She hesitated, her cheeks flushed, uncertain just how she felt, except that she was surprised to find eager acceptance uppermost in her mind at the moment. 'I don't—I mean, you don't have to bother, Alexei.'

He regarded her steadily. 'You would prefer that I get Paolo to help you, perhaps?' he asked softly, and Storm stared at him open-mouthed for a moment, then held the frilled neck of the robe close under her chin and swept past him into her room. She spun round swiftly a second later when she heard the door close and found him standing just inside, those glittering blue eyes challenging her to deny his right to be there.

'You must hurry,' he told her quietly. 'There is not very much time before our guest arrives.'

'He's English.'

She realised as she spoke that she made it sound like an accusation, and she thought she saw the corners of his wide mouth twist in ironic amusement. 'You do not sound very pleased about meeting a fellow countryman.'

'You didn't tell me he was English.'

'No, I did not.'

'Even though you must have known I would be glad to see someone from my own country.'

The cool blue eyes regarded her steadily for a moment, and she could not have sworn just what was going on behind that Slavonic-looking mask. 'I did not think a business acquaintance of mine would interest you to that extent.'

'Oh!'

He was obviously thinking deeply about some-

157

thing, and she watched him surreptitiously from the shadow of her lashes, wondering what was on his mind. 'I want you to understand, Storm,' he said at last, slowly and as if he considered every word before he said it. 'As far as Sir Gerald Gordon is concerned it could be very useful that I have an English wife.'

'Oh, I see.' She met his eyes for a moment or two and hastily smothered the bitter feeling of resentment she felt at the idea of being used to further his business interests. 'Well, I'm glad I'm useful for something in your estimation!'

She had not meant it to sound quite so bitter, and she saw a brief hint of surprise in his eyes before he frowned. 'Please do not be sarcastic, Storm, it is not becoming, and quite uncalled for.'

'I think I——'

'I hope, for this evening at least, that you can remember you are married to me and not to Paolo. It will create a better impression if you do.'

Storm felt the colour flooding into her cheeks and she clenched her hands into tight little fists at her sides. He had said very little on the way home about finding her with Paolo, but it looked as if he now intended making up for it. Despite the unlikelihood of it, she had nurtured a little spark of hope that part of his annoyance was prompted by jealousy; now it seemed it was strictly fear for the impression it would make on a business acquaintance.

'You have no call to talk to me like that, Alexei,' she told him shakily. 'It's unfair and quite without foundation to suspect me as you do.'

He looked down at her coolly, it seemed, although something in his manner set her own pulses pounding crazily, as if in anticipation. 'In view of the situation in which I found you only a very short time ago, I think I have every right to talk to you like that,' he told her shortly. 'It was fortunate that my aunt was able to tell me where to find you, for it would have made a very unfortunate impression upon our guest had you arrived home late for dinner, looking as if you were returning from a rendezvous with a lover, and in the company of my cousin.'

'Oh—oh, you—you—I don't *care* what impression I make on your precious guest! I don't care what *any*one thinks—or—or if—oh, you—you——' Words tumbled over one another, but failed miserably to make any sort of sense, and her green eyes blazed at him furiously.

'Well, it matters to me!' The cold voice cut across her tirade. 'And you will behave like a reasonable adult in front of my guest, no matter what childish tantrums you indulge in in your bedroom.'

'You—you—monster!'

Her breathing was wild and erratic and she stepped back hastily when he came across the room towards her. 'As you please,' he said quietly, and his hands reached out for the tie at the neck of her robe. 'Now please do not waste any more time, Storm. It is getting late and I want you downstairs ready to meet Sir Gerald when he arrives.'

Storm felt dismayingly close to tears, but she could see the futility of further argument with him. He was bound to be the victor, for she could not deny that she had been in a compromising enough position to anger any husband, and he had seen her with his own eyes. To have found her like that would have been a blow to his pride and he would not be quick to forgive.

'I can help myself, thank you!' She knocked away his hands, refusing to have him help her, at least at this stage. The robe parted and she had it half-way down her arms when she paused, suddenly conscious of the little she wore under it. 'You——'

'Si, abrighi!' he ordered curtly, and the robe was pulled forcibly from her arms and thrown carelessly across the bed. 'Stop seeking excuses, Storm, and get dressed, or I shall lose all patience with you!'

She would have argued that he had done so already, but the tissue-fine silk slip she wore clung closely to the contours of her body and exposed a smooth expanse of pale gold skin above the low-cut lacy top, and she felt suddenly very vulnerable with those icy blue eyes on her.

She turned hastily and reached for the jade green dress he wanted her to wear. It slipped easily over her head and she slid her arms into the brief sleeves, then reached behind her with both hands in an attempt to close that elusive zip. In a moment, however, Alexei was round behind her, brushing her hands impatiently aside.

'I am here to help you,' he reminded her. 'Must you be so difficult, Storm?'

'I'm not being difficult, I——' She swung round, half way to facing him, but he gripped her upper arms roughly and turned her back again.

'I promise you that if I lose my temper you will be very, very sorry,' he warned. 'Now please make some attempt to co-operate. I am trying to help you!'

'Thank you!'

She sounded meek and very quiet, in direct contrast to the chaos that was going on inside her. She could feel the warmth from his body on the nakedness of her back as he stood close behind her, and his fingers touching her skin was like a touch of fire. Instinctively she closed her eyes on the wild, incredible longings that his touch aroused in her, banishing everything else from her mind.

'Keep still!'

Inadvertently she had swayed slightly, and the deep-voiced command made her stiffen hastily, reminding her that he was impatient with her, anxious for her to be ready to welcome his important guest. Nothing would be further from his mind than the effect he was having on her.

'I'm—I'm sorry, Alexei.'

'You are a capricious and perplexing woman,' he accused. 'And I do not begin to understand you!'

'Have you tried?' Her voice had an oddly husky sound, and she felt him pause in his task.

'I have tried,' he said quietly. His long brown fingers slid softly along the length of her spine as the zip closed together, and she shivered. 'Are you cold?' he asked.

'No, no, of course not!'

Her hands were curled tightly and the pulse at her temple almost blinded her with its throbbing, but she did not move, only stood there, close to the strong warmth of him and almost praying aloud for him to put his arms around her. She wanted that to happen more than anything else in the world at the moment.

'You look very beautiful.' He spoke softly and startlingly close to her ear, so that his breath stirred the tendrils of hair on her neck, and her heart responded so violently that her head swam with it. Then he bent his head and pressed his lips lightly to the soft skin of her neck, moving aside the tawny gold hair with caressing fingers, his dark head brushing softly against her face.

'Alexei!' She whispered his name, wanting him to know how she felt, but half afraid he would find her wild emotions a subject for scorn.

'*Si, amante?*' He too spoke softly, and his arms slid around her at last, turning her slowly within their circle until she looked up into the strong, carved bronze face with its light eyes. Eyes that no longer looked cold and icy but darker with some deep passion that made her shiver with anticipation. He had never spoken to her so often in Italian as he had today, and she told herself it was a good omen, a sign that he no longer considered her a stranger.

'I—I wish I——'

She shook her head, too unsure of herself and of him to tell him how she felt and how sorry she was that she had gone off with Paolo as she had, and he smiled. That rare and gentle smile that softened the stern lines of his face and made him look so much more approachable and less overpowering. She had seen him smile at Gino like that, and once or twice at Lisetta, but never before at her, and the effect of it was breathtaking.

He held her close and studied her for a long moment with those light blue eyes. *'Amante mia!'* he said softly. He pulled her closer, until her body was crushed against his own muscular strength and she could feel the tense, exciting warmth of him through her thin gown, and the steady, strong beat of his heart, faster than normal, under the spread of her fingers.

'Alexei!'

She whispered his name, with his mouth touching hers, his lips brushing lightly, teasingly against hers until she wanted to cry out to him. Her whole being ached for his lean, hard body to possess her completely, for the strong brown hands to caress her passionately, urgent with the same consuming desires that burned in her.

He made a sound that was almost a moan, a soft indescribable sound, and her head was forced back as his mouth became suddenly more hard and dominant, possessed of a fierce hunger that swept Storm along on a tide of elation and excitement she could not hope to control.

'*Carissima! Po' amante mia!*' Soft Italian words, whispered against her ear as he lifted her into his arms and carried her across to the bed, his voice deep and husky with a passion barely contained.

He turned swiftly, his eyes glittering, when a soft knocking sounded at the bedroom door, and he laid her gently down and looked at her curiously, bringing his mind back to immediate things with a shake of his dark head.

Storm sat there on the edge of the lace-trimmed bed, her lips parted, hating whoever it was that had disturbed them with an intensity that frightened her. 'It—it could be Clemente,' she whispered, but Alexei was frowning, almost as if he suspected who was on the other side of the door.

'Storm! *Carissima!*'

The voice was scarcely above a whisper, obviously hoping to remain unheard except to her, but there was no mistaking to whom it belonged, and Storm closed her eyes on the agonising irony of it. Paolo had never before ventured to come to her room, and he had to choose this moment to come knocking and whispering at her door. Who could help but suspect an intrigue, a prearranged meeting? Certainly not Alexei, not after the scene he had witnessed earlier at Pompeii, and her heart sank coldly into a void of hopelessness.

She knew, even before she looked at him, what she

would see on Alexei's face, and she could have cried aloud at the harshness, the stark fury, she saw there. He looked down at her, and from the expression in those cold eyes, she knew he was despising himself for succumbing to a moment of weakness, as much as her for her deception, as he saw it.

'It seems I have been made a fool of,' he said in a cold hard voice. 'I congratulate you, *signora*. It is not easy to make a fool of Alexei Romano.'

'Alexei, I——'

But he was in no mood to listen and brushed aside her attempt to explain with one disdainful hand. The tenderness, the passion of a few moments before had been wiped out as if they had never existed. 'I hope you do not find my presence in your bedroom too much of an embarrassment.' He turned on his heel and strode to the door, flinging it wide.

'Alexei!' Her cry followed him and reached Paolo, who stood beyond in the gallery, staring at his cousin in disbelief.

'*Madre di Dio!*' he breathed piously, realising his blunder, but Storm ignored him, her eyes following Alexei, dark with unhappiness and bright with unshed tears.

He turned in the doorway, his arrogant dark head in deep contrast to the white wall behind him. 'I hope you are as adept at playing charades when you meet our guest,' he said coldly, ignoring Paolo as if he did not exist. 'I would prefer to have Sir Gerald convinced that our marriage is at least normally tolerable. If that is not imposing too much upon you.'

'Oh, Alexei, please don't!' She was almost in tears and her eyes looked huge and shinily green in the yellow light from the overhead lamps, but he remained unmoved.

'I shall expect you downstairs in the *salotto* in five minutes' time,' he said shortly, and turned and strode off along the carpeted gallery.

There was a heavy, meaningful silence for several moments after he had gone, and Storm thought she had never in her life felt so utterly lost and helpless. No matter if Alexei had been prepared to forget her previous indiscretion in those few wonderful minutes just now, there was little likelihood of his ever doing so again, and she had only herself and Paolo to blame.

'Oh, *cara mia*, I am so sorry!' Paolo's dark eyes looked unbelievably contrite, and it was very difficult to become really angry with him, especially when her own eyes were brimming with tears.

'How could you, Paolo? How could you come to my room like that? You've never, ever done it before, why now?'

'*Cara*, I did not know, how *could* I know, that Alexei was with you? He too has never been to your bedroom before, has he? Not since your marriage?'

Storm shook her head miserably. 'It was the first time, and—oh, Paolo, what am I going to do?'

His shrug was instinctive rather than uncaring,

and he reached out and brushed away a tear from her cheek with one gentle finger. 'There is no time for you to do anything at the moment, *piccola*,' he reminded her softly. 'You have to hide your tears and be downstairs in less than three minutes. We will straighten it all out when our important visitor is gone, no?'

Storm looked at her wristwatch through a blur of tears and nodded. 'I—I suppose so,' she said huskily. 'I—I don't know if I can, Paolo.'

'Oh, Storm! *Graziosa mia*, you look so sad!' He leaned across and kissed her lightly on her forehead. 'Does Alexei's anger mean so much to you?' It was quite the wrong thing to have said in the circumstances and the tears flowed anew down her face, tears she was unable to check, and Paolo pulled her to him, her face against his shoulder, rubbing one hand soothingly over her bowed head. 'Oh, *cara mia*, please don't cry so! Shall I tell them that you have a bad headache and cannot come down to dinner?'

'Oh no, no!' She pushed away from him, brushing a hand across her eyes. 'I must go down! Alexei will never forgive me if I don't!'

Sir Gerald Gordon proved to be both charming and garrulous, and in this instance Storm was very glad not to have to make much effort to entertain him. For one thing he seemed quite delighted with the company of the Contessa, and also he was something of a story-teller and seemed to have an endless repertoire of anecdotes. Her own rather unhappy silence, she thought, went unnoticed, except by Alexei.

From time to time she tried to catch his eye down the length of the table, but each time he avoided looking at her, and she found it increasingly difficult to maintain her appearance of calm when he was so persistently cool and hostile. Dinner seemed to go on endlessly and all the time she was afraid she would cry, sooner or later, and stand even less chance of seeing Alexei relent.

It was towards the end of the meal that Sir Gerald looked at Storm with a smile of polite enquiry. 'Will you be visiting the old country with your husband when he comes to see us next month, Signora Romano?' he asked, and Storm blinked for a moment in confusion.

Alexei had said nothing to her about going to England and she was very uncertain how she should answer, but the very idea of visiting her old home again in the near future gave her spirits a sudden lift, and she looked down the length of the table at Alexei with wide, hopeful eyes.

'I—I'm not sure, Sir Gerald,' she said. 'Alexei——'

'I think not, Sir Gerald.' Alexei's deep, quiet voice cut across her question. 'My wife has to stay and look after my young nephew. He is my ward, you will remember, and not really old enough to be taken on what is after all purely a business trip. I shall be in England no more than two days at most, and it is scarcely worth all the disturbance it would cause.'

Storm felt as if he had dealt her a physical blow, and she could only stare at him in blank dismay for several seconds before hastily looking down again. There was no limit, it seemed, to Alexei's thirst for revenge, and she fought wildly with the sudden aching desire to get up from the table and run out of the room, regardless of the impression it made on their guest.

'Ah yes, of course,' Sir Gerald murmured politely, obviously impressed by his host's single-mindedness. 'Pleasure and business don't mix, eh, Romano? And a wife is happiest in her own home! Well, the old ways have a lot to recommend them. I regret the passing of some of those old ideals, I can tell you, my dear chap!'

Storm could feel the curious eyes of the Contessa on her, but she dared not look up at her or she knew she would have weakened beyond control. Later, she knew, the Contessa would ask her all about it. Why Alexei had been so deliberately callous, and she would have to try and find the words to explain.

'Old-fashioned standards have very little meaning now,' Alexei said. 'Even to wives.' He looked directly down the table at Storm, an icy glint in his eyes telling her that the jibe was intended for her. She had never before seen him so deliberately cruel and she found it incredibly hard to bear.

Sir Gerald shook his grey head in regret. 'Well,

I'm very glad to see such a complete and happy family circle in your home, my dear Romano. I'm always impressed by a happy family atmosphere; it tells me a lot about a man if his home life is in good order.'

Such a glaring misconception was almost too much for Storm, and she held her two hands tightly together for a moment, trying to still their trembling. Somehow, soon, she must get away from this coolly polite atmosphere and give way to her own pent-up feelings, or she would burst.

But it was only when they got up from the table that her chance came. Alexei and Paolo apparently had some business to discuss with their guest, and they went off to the study together, leaving the three women alone. The Contessa and Signora Veronese went downstairs to the big drawing-room with Storm, but she was in no mood for small-talk, and she saw Alexei's absence as her chance to escape at last.

'If you'll excuse me,' she said, 'I'll just go and see if Gino's settled down to sleep.'

Signora Veronese might possibly have been fooled by her excuse, but the Contessa certainly was not, and she turned anxious eyes on her, gently concerned for her obvious unhappiness. 'Storm, *cara*, what is wrong?'

Had they been alone, Storm would not have hesitated to confide in her, but the cold, malicious presence of Signora Veronese deterred her, and she merely shook her head, feeling the threat of tears again, prickling at the back of her eyes and choking her throat. She had never, she felt certain, ever been so abjectly miserable in her life.

'Is it not obvious what is wrong, Lisetta?' Signora Veronese asked in her harsh voice, before Storm could find the words to answer. 'To be discovered by one's husband in the act of seducing another man must surely be disturbing to even the most brazen, although I for one can find little pity in my heart for such a woman!'

'*Nome di Dio*, Sofia! You would not find it in your hard heart to pity a starving child!' The Contessa's defence was swift and fierce, and Storm felt grateful to her for her unflinching support, but she still desired nothing more than the chance to flee to her own room.

Lisetta Berenetti, however, having taken up cudgels on her behalf, was not yet ready to relinquish the fight, and her dark eyes blazed below the brightness of her red hair. 'As for your *prezioso* —your *bambino*—huh! He is the seducer, Sofia Veronese, and well you know it! He has the eye of the Romanos, that one!'

'*Silenzio!*' Signora Veronese's harsh features were twisted into a caricature of themselves with the violent emotions that tore at her, and her voice was barely above a whisper. 'You dare to speak so of my Paolo when you are no better than a——'

'*Basta*, Sofia, *per favore*,' the Contessa told her quietly, although her dark eyes shone with anger. 'Do not say something you will be sorry for!'

'Oh, please,' Storm begged, her voice choking in her throat as she listened to the bitterness between the two women. 'Don't quarrel because of me! Please don't!'

Signora Veronese's black eyes switched to her, sharp with malice, narrowed and burning with a hatred that Storm could not fully understand. 'Alexei should never have married a foreign woman—a *domestica*!' The harsh voice spat scorn at Storm's original position in the household as she saw it.

'Signora Veronese, I—I know you dislike me——' Storm began, but was given no chance to complete the sentence before that harsh voice cut her short again, thick with venom.

'I despise you, *signora*! You are no fit wife for a Romano and Alexei, I think, is at last beginning to see what a fool he has been. Now perhaps he will annul this ridiculous mockery of a marriage and send you away before the name of Romano is further disgraced by having English blood too passed on to its descendants!'

'So!' The Contessa's tight little smile understood at last, and Storm too saw a glimmer of light. The reason why Signora Veronese hated her so much. 'You hated poor gloomy Natasha, did you not, Sofia? Because she brought Russian blood to your precious Romanos, and now you fear that Alexei's sons will shame you further by being partly English!'

Signora Veronese's sharp chin angled defiantly,

her eyes glittering as much hatred for the woman who faced her as for the absent Natasha Romano. 'The Romanos,' she declared coldly, 'were a proud old Italian family, and will be so again!'

'When you have your Paolo safely installed, *si*, Sofia?' the Contessa asked softly. 'Oh, I can see so clearly now what it is you want. Benito did not marry, so his poor little Gino is not a Romano, and while Alexei had no wife Paolo was safe as the heir to all that Luigi and Alexei have built here!'

It was obvious that the Contessa's estimate of the situation was an accurate one, and also that the Signora resented it bitterly, for her black eyes looked from Storm to the Contessa with a chilling, virulent hatred that made Storm shiver.

'Paolo has a right to it all,' she said coldly, and fiercely. 'He is the only *real* Romano left! He has no foreign blood, nor will he marry beneath his station for the sake of some stupid servant girl's honour!' Her gaze raked scornfully over Storm from top to toe. 'But I have faith in the sense of duty of the Romanos, even in Alexei. He may have married a *domestica*, but he will not disgrace his name by letting her bear his sons, I would swear to it!'

'Oh, please, please!' Storm put her hands to her ears, her faced flushed and crumpled with threatening tears, shaking her head violently from side to side. 'Paolo can *have* it all! I don't care! You're right, *signora*, there'll be no sons, not mine and Alexei's, not now. Paolo made sure of that!' She held her hands together in front of her in a tight ball, her body shaken with sobs. 'I—I'm going away, as far as I can get, from you, from Paolo, from—from Alexei! I never want to see any of you again. Never, never, never!'

She did not stop to heed the Contessa's entreating hands, outstretched to her, nor to see the gloating satisfaction in Signora Veronese's black eyes, but ran from the room and on up the marble stairs to the long gallery above, seeking the sanctuary of her own room. She felt abused and humiliated, obliged to face the fact that what the Signora said was probably true.

Alexei would never treat her as a proper wife, not even for the sake of carrying on his ancient name. He could do that by adoping Gino, as the Contessa had said he meant to do, and Gino, at least, was all Italian. Even Signora Veronese could not contest that.

It was instinctive that she went into Gino's room first when she got upstairs, and she found him peacefully asleep. Smoothing back the black hair genly from his forehead as he slept, she cried softly to herself while she decided her own future.

She would miss Gino, she would miss her life at the Villa, no matter how unsettled it had been at times, but most of all she knew she would miss Alexei. She had known in the first few moments of their meeting that he was a man she would not easily forget, but she had not for a moment anticipated becoming so closely involved with him.

Now she found it hard to visualise a life without him, but she knew that if she stayed on here she would be living in a fool's paradise if she hoped ever to see him as warm and passionate again as he had been for those few minutes tonight. Now that he was convinced of her preference for Paolo, nothing would change his mind. That facet of his character had been one of the first things she recognised in him.

She walked into her own room and, without turning on the light, walked across to the window and pressed her forehead to the cool window glass. He would most likely have their brief marriage annulled; there was certainly no legal impediment to his doing so.

She pressed her face harder to the shiny coolness of the window and wept for something she had never really had, while outside the bright moonlight shimmered on the smooth bay, and down in the garden the shading trees stood darkly wavering in the soft wind that blew in from the sea.

Bellabaia—beautiful bay, the place she had thought a paradise on earth only a few short months ago, and which she had expected to see for only two short weeks, during a holiday. If only she had not spoken to a good-looking stranger and a little boy!

CHAPTER NINE

Iᴛ took Storm quite a few moments to persuade the
Contessa to ring for a taxi for her, to take her to the
airport, and she begged her not to tell Alexei that
she had gone until there was no way of keeping it
from him. That way she had the idea that she could
perhaps be well on the way to England before he
knew. Of course it was most likely, after his treatment of her tonight, that he would not care where
she was, but he might just feel sufficiently slighted
at the idea of being deserted to follow and make
her come back.

The Contessa had not pleaded with her, as she
had half expected she would. She had asked her,
quietly, what had upset her so much before dinner,
and she explained as best she could, how that fate-
ful afternoon and evening had evolved. The Contessa shook her head, but said little, and Storm had
the feeling that probably she had seen this parting
as inevitable sooner or later.

She had kissed her gently on both cheeks and
given the taxi driver instructions to take her to the
airport, and then gone back into the villa with
scarcely a backward glance, leaving Storm feeling
finally and utterly deserted.

The drive in the taxi, along the moonlit road to
Naples, reminded her of when she had driven

along there with Paolo, and she felt the hot, salty sting of tears again. The citrus groves, so sweetly scented, and with their little straw roofs to protect them from inclement weather. The dark glow of the sea below the terraced cliffs, it was all so heart-achingly familiar suddenly, and she knew she could not stop herself from crying again.

She would arrive at the airport looking forlorn, and very much like what she was—a runaway wife. Desperately, as they ran into the airport approach, she sought in her handbag for make-up to disguise the ravages wrought by tears, using the dim interior light of the taxi to do the repairs.

Her reflection in the handbag mirror appalled her. Her eyes looked huge, and dismayingly red-rimmed, and her face was as pale as death with no trace of the hurriedly applied lipstick left on her mouth. It was hard to imagine that the ghostlike creature who stared at her from the mirror was the same girl who only hours before had been delirious with delight when her husband made love to her.

She had left the jade green dress on the bed, a memento of her brief happiness that she had had no room to bring with her. Her packing had been done in haste and she would not have crumpled and spoiled the gown for anything.

She faced the fact now, that she had so far avoided admitting, even to herself. She loved Alexei in a way she had never dreamed was possible, and far too much to stay and be a make-believe wife only. She had loved him even before she agreed to marry him, for surely no enlightened modern girl would have accepted such a marriage on such flimsy grounds if she had not been blinded by her own feelings.

It would have been enough to save her own reputation if she had simply left the villa, there and then, and gone back to England, she could see that quite clearly now. But she had wanted to stay and she had taken any opportunity offered, no matter what the conditions. Alexei had probably meant to dispense with her in time, anyway, when it suited his book.

She took a last look at herself and a great shuddering sigh escaped her as she closed the clasp of her handbag and looked out at the bright, busy bustle of the airport. The taxi driver was probably already curious about her and the sound of her sigh prompted him to turn briefly and look at her over one shoulder.

'*Signora?*'

Storm shook her head. 'Nothing—I'm sorry.'

'*Si, signora!*'

She thought he was more than curious about her, having had that brief glimpse of her tear-stained face, and she wondered if she would have the nerve to mingle with the others in the crowded terminal, but at least in a crowd she would be less conspicuous.

The man accepted the generous tip she gave him and touched his cap, his dark eyes surreptitiously studying her while he took her suitcases from his taxi. He knew who she was, for she had heard her own name among the Italian instructions that the Contessa had given him, and she was suspicious that his mind was working along obvious lines.

'Thank you, I can manage now.'

He looked down at her two suitcases, the same ones she had brought from England with her. '*Due scatole, signora? Con permesso——*'

'No, no, please, I can manage! Thank you.' She was anxious to be on her way. To disappear into the faceless crowd in the terminal; out here she felt somehow vulnerable, and she picked up her cases, while the driver shrugged resignedly and watched her disappear into the crowded and brightly lit building.

It must have been her pale face and red-rimmed eyes, Storm told herself, that made the ticket clerk look at her so oddly, and she wished she could have done a better job of disguising the signs of her distress. She did not mind how she got to England, she told him, as long as it was on a plane that left very soon, but the clerk was shaking his sleek black head regretfully.

'*Mi spiace*, Signora Romano,' he said. 'There is nothing for—two hours.'

'Two hours?' Storm stared at him in dismay, her heart racing in panic, her anxiety to be away even more urgent when she thought of Alexei knowing she was gone long before two hours from now.

'*Mi spiace, signora!*'

'But isn't there one to—to—oh, somewhere!'

She could feel those persistent tears about to start again and dreaded making a fool of herself in a place as public as Naples airport, and the clerk was already looking at her as if he too feared an exhibition he would have to cope with.

'*Signora*, it seems you are distressed.' He used his hands to convey a good deal more than he said. 'I will call a young lady to help you. Perhaps the *signora* would care to rest for a while, in private, *si?*'

He was kind, but anxious to have her transferred to some other responsibility, and she nodded wearily. 'I—I really don't feel very well, *signore*, if I could——'

'*Si, si, certo, signora!*'

She was shown into a small, quiet room furnished with two armchairs and a small desk and chair which, she felt sure, was not normally available to passengers, and she looked enquiringly at her guide when she opened the door.

'Is—is it all right for me to be here?' she asked, and the girl nodded, smiling understandingly.

'Oh *si, certo*, Signora Romano!'

The use of her full name gave her the clue as to why she was privileged and she hesitated only briefly before nodding her thanks. She might as well make the most of being Alexei Romano's wife, just this once. 'Thank you,' she said, and the girl smiled briefly.

'*Prego, non ne parli, signora.*'

With a bob of her head the girl was gone and

Storm was alone in the quiet little room. It was then that she realised that she had not booked herself a seat on that plane that left in two hours from now. The armchair she sat in was comfortable and suddenly she felt very, very tired, so she leaned back her head and told herself that it could do no harm to rest for a moment or two before going to book her seat. Such an emotional upheaval as she had just gone through could be incredibly exhausting and she needed time to gather herself together again.

She had not meant to go to sleep, but she realised as she opened her eyes that she must have done just that. The little room felt stuffy and she stretched her arms above her head to restore the circulation to them, glancing at her wristwatch as she did so. Thirty minutes of one of those two hours had passed already and she felt much less distressed.

A glance into her handbag mirror confirmed that she looked better too. True, her eyes were still rimmed with crying, but they looked much less obvious and her cheeks had more colour, but there was still a dark, sad look about her green eyes and she wondered how she would face up to life as a working girl again.

She would, of course, revert to her maiden name and so save Alexei any embarrassment when he came to England, but she looked down at the heavy gold ring on her marriage finger with regret. She would return the ring to him after she got back.

In a reverie between sleepiness and nostalgia, she

could have started crying again, but she pulled herself up sharply and got to her feet, determined to be practical. A light, tentative tap at the door made her spin round swiftly and she almost breathed a sigh of relief when the dark pretty face of the airport stewardess smiled at her warily.

'*Signora——*' she began, then stepped back hastily when someone brushed past her, striding purposefully into the little room as if he owned it, and sweeping all before him, as always.

'*Vade via, per favore, signorina!*' he told the stewardess, and the girl, after one brief uncertain glance at Storm, nodded her head and hastily withdrew.

'*Si, signore!*'

For a long moment after the door closed after her Alexei stood there, just inside the door, looking at her, and Storm kept her back to him. Those tears would surely get the better of her now again. 'May I ask why you saw fit to walk out of a dinner that you knew was very important to me?' he asked then, and she did not answer.

It did not matter apparently that she was unhappy, too unhappy to go on living in the same house with him, he was only concerned with his own affairs. He waited for several seconds and when she did not answer he spoke again to her unfriendly back.

'I think I am entitled to an answer,' he said quietly.

'I—I'm sorry.'

Her voice was husky and not much more than a whisper, and she heard him move closer, presumably to enable him to hear what she said. 'You realise that your—your running away like this has probably cost me a great deal of money, and an important business contract in England?'

Money and business, Storm thought wildly, the only things he ever cared about, according to Paolo, and it looked as if Paolo was right. Anger suddenly rose uppermost in her tangled emotions and her hands were clenched tightly as she turned to face him, her green eyes blazing, her cheeks flushed.

'Is it so important to you?' she asked, her voice shaking with both anger and those pent-up tears. 'Do you want to buy England as well as most of Italy? Does nothing else matter to you?'

He said nothing for a second, but those icy blue eyes were far from being as cold and chilling as she expected, and the firm, straight mouth was not set like an angry line as she had often seen it. 'I would not be here if that were so,' he said quietly, and Storm looked at him warily.

Her lips were parted and her eyes huge and green as she tried to decide just what he meant. 'I— I don't understand,' she said.

The immaculate white jacket, she noticed for the first time, was open and there was an unusually untidy look about his dark hair where it fell across his forehead. 'I am assured by Lisetta that Paolo has never—has never been to your room before.'

'No, no, he hasn't,' she said, in a small quiet voice, not daring to hope that he was going to admit he had been wrong.

'It seems that I owe you an apology for that.'

She waved her hands to dismiss it as unimportant, but she knew what it would have cost him to apologise. 'Oh, it doesn't matter,' she said, and realised, suddenly, how incredibly weary she sounded. Then she looked up at him briefly. 'I'm—I'm sorry about your business deal, but you shouldn't have come—not for me, not when it was so important to you.'

'You do not think that having my wife desert me is important?'

She felt her heart leap suddenly. Even the faintest hint that he cared was enough to set her pulses racing and she told herself she was a gullible fool. 'I didn't mean you to follow me. I hoped I'd be gone by the time you realised.'

'Lisetta knew there was no flight for England for over two hours, she made sure of that before she rang for your taxi.' His wide, straight mouth tipped briefly at one corner in a hint of a smile. 'The name of Romano carries some weight around here. I drove as fast as I could, and I'm afraid Sir Gerald is rather puzzled by my behaviour.'

Storm shook her head, her eyes wide and uncertain. 'You—you left him? To come and find me?'

He nodded. 'Of course. It is a matter of pride when a man's wife deserts him.'

'I see.' She looked down at her hands again. 'I'm—I'm sorry, but I was—upset.'

'The quarrel with my aunt?' he asked, and she nodded.

'I'm afraid Signora Veronese doesn't like me,' she said. 'She despises me for a—a *domestica*, and I don't have to have that translated!' She smiled ruefully, but failed to find a response on that serious face. 'I—I suppose my pride was hurt.'

'I can understand that. Pride is not the sole prerogative of the wealthy or the aristocratic. You have as much right to yours as anyone else.'

It was unexpected to hear him being so agreeable, and she laughed uneasily. 'I'm afraid your aunt doesn't share your view, and as I'm married to you she's—she was afraid——' She stopped there, unwilling to go into the intimate details of Signor Veronese's tirade.

The unfailing sense of excitement that he had always aroused in her was coursing through her body now, like an irresistible fire, and she wished he would either go and leave her, or make some move to satisfy her longing for him. It would be impossible, she thought, for her ever to forget Alexei, no matter how long she was away from him.

The blue eyes held hers for a brief moment before she hastily lowered her own gaze. 'If my aunt and Paolo were to go away,' he said quietly, 'would you come back, Storm?'

She did not answer, she could not, for several

moments, her heart was hammering so insistently at her ribs that she had a strange breathless feeling. Then she shook her head, slowly and with such obvious reluctance that he must have realised it. 'I —I couldn't, Alexei.'

At once the blue eyes took on that cold, icy look she had hoped never to see again, and there was a faint flush on the high Slavonic-looking cheeks. 'Because I speak of sending Paolo away?' he asked, and Storm looked up hastily, anxious to deny that at least.

'Oh no! How could you still think Paolo means anything to me?'

'Then why will you not come back?'

She simply stood there for several moments with her head bowed. How did she tell a man she could not come back and live with him because she loved him too much? It must surely be the most ironic situation any woman ever found herself in.

'Storm?' He spoke her name softly, and its gentleness, the hint of anxiety she thought she detected in his voice was her undoing. Great rolling tears coursed down her cheeks and she brushed them away impatiently with a clenched hand.

'I—I can't come back, Alexei, be-because I love you.'

There, it was said, and he could now realise how she felt, why she could not go on as she had been. He must surely understand now, but he neither spoke nor moved for a full minute.

'Then come home, *carissima*,' he said softly.

'Alexei!' She looked up at him, wide-eyed, not daring to believe that she really saw that warm, exciting glow in those light eyes as they looked at her.

He moved then, reaching out his arms for her and drawing her close to the lean hardness of his body as if he would crush her until she was part of him, and she could feel the warmth of his flesh and the throbbing beat of his heart through the white frilled shirt. She leaned her face against his heart, but he pulled back her head by the length of her tawny hair, and found her mouth.

Even in those few unforgettable moments in her bedroom he had not kissed her like that, and she felt as if every fibre in her body was responding to his touch. A fierce, erotic sensation that made her moan softly as he caressed her, his mouth drawing the very breath from her, until her head spun with a kind of wonderful delirium.

'Storm! *Bella Tempesta mia! Carissima!*' His voice, deep and soft, breathed warmly against her mouth, her neck and the soft vulnerable base of her throat, the strong brown hands unbelievably gentle as they caressed her. 'You will come back, *mia bella*, will you not?'

Storm looked up at him with bright, shining green eyes, her tawny head tipped back as she smiled at him. 'You know I will,' she told him. 'I don't really know if I could have gone when it came to the point. I love you, my darling Alexei. I think I always have.'

'Always?' He looked down at her with a small

doubting frown between his brows. 'You were never—that way about Paolo?'

'Never,' she denied firmly. 'I knew Paolo wasn't serious about me either, but he was good company, especially when my husband seemed determined to ignore me.' She kissed that firm, square chin and laughed softly in her new-found confidence. 'He said you didn't deserve me.'

'Perhaps I did not,' Alexei admitted with uncharacteristic modesty. 'But I loved you and I would never have let Paolo take you from me. If you—if you had loved him enough——' He stopped, and his reticence surprised Storm so much so that she looked at him anxiously for a moment.

'*Caro?*' she prompted him gently, the Italian endearment coming easily to her lips, and he drew her close again, holding her so tightly that she could not have moved even had she wanted to, his mouth urgent with the fierce hunger that thrilled her so.

'If you had loved him enough, *carissima*,' he said quietly, 'I think perhaps I might have let you go, if it would have made you happy, and if you had begged me to.'

'Oh no, my love!' She pressed her lips to that small throbbing pulse on his throat that she had always noticed when he was moved or aroused, even to anger. 'There was never any question of that, and Paolo could never have married me, anyway. Signora Veronese has plans for Paolo to provide the Romano line with the Italian sons she thinks it should have.'

For a moment he was silent, then that fascinating, bronze carved face looked down at her earnestly. 'She has said all these things to you, *carissima*?'

Storm nodded. 'The Contessa was there too.'

'And you ran away because you loved me and you thought——'

She traced the shape of that firm mouth with one finger. 'I thought your aunt might possibly be right,' she said softly. 'That you had married me because both our reputations were at stake, but that you would never allow me——'

'*Si, cara mia?*' he prompted gently, and the blue eyes looked down at her with an expression that robbed her of any false modesty.

'She was quite sure you would never allow me to bear your sons and disgrace the Romano name with English blood.'

'*Cagna!*' The venom in the one word startled her and she looked up at him curious and wide-eyed. To her surprise he laughed, only the second time she had ever heard him do so. 'I am being very uncomplimentary to my Aunt Sofia, *carissima mia*!' His fingers undid the buttons of her coat and the two at the neck of her dress and slid the soft material from her shoulder, then he bent his head and put his lips to the soft warmth of her flesh. 'We will show Aunt Sofia whether or not you will bear my sons,' he whispered softly. 'We will go home now, *amante mia*, and soon Paolo will have

189

no hope of being the provider of the Romano line, hmm?'

'Even if I'm not Italian?' Storm asked, her shining eyes showing that she knew the answer to that well enough.

'*Silenzio!*' Alexei said firmly, and Storm was content with that.

Mills & Boon Classics

The very best of Mills & Boon
romances, brought back for those of you
who missed reading them when they
were first published.

There are three other Classics for you to collect this
September

NO FRIEND OF MINE
by Lilian Peake

Lester Kings was her brother's friend, not hers, Elise told herself
firmly. She had never liked him when she was a child, and now
he had come back into their lives the old antagonism was there
still, as strong as ever. Yet somehow she just couldn't stop
thinking about him . . .

SHADE OF THE PALMS
by Roberta Leigh

To Stephen Brandon, Julia was no more than Miss Watson, his
unflappable, highly efficient secretary. A dowdy woman wearing
unfashionable clothes, sensible shoes and spectacles, he would
have thought if he'd considered the matter at all. But he was to
discover that appearances can be deceptive and that there was a
totally unexpected side to Julia . . .

THE ARROGANCE OF LOVE
by Anne Mather

Dominic Halstad was the most attractive man Susan had ever
met, and made her rather difficult fiancé David seem dull by
comparison. But even if her first loyalty were not to David, what
right had she to think about Dominic — a married man?

If you have difficulty in obtaining any of these books through
your local paperback retailer, write to:

Mills & Boon Reader Service
P.O. Box 236, Thornton Road, Croydon, Surrey, CR9 3RU.

Mills & Boon Classics

The very best of Mills & Boon
romances, brought back for those of you
who missed reading them when they
were first published.

In
October
we bring back the following four
great romantic titles.

NO QUARTER ASKED
by Janet Dailey

Stacy Adams was a rich girl who wanted to sample real life for
a change, so she courageously took herself off alone to Texas
for a while. It was obvious from the first that the arrogant
rancher Cord Harris, for some reason, disapproved of her — but
why should she care what he thought?

MIRANDA'S MARRIAGE
by Margery Hilton

Desperation forced Miranda to encamp for the night in Jason
Steele's office suite, but unfortunately he found her there, and
after the unholy wrath that resulted she never dreamed that a
few months later she would become his wife. For Jason was
reputed to be a rake where women were concerned. So what
chance of happiness had Miranda?

THE LIBRARY TREE
by Lilian Peake

Carolyn Lyle was the niece of a very influential man, and
nothing would convince her new boss, that iceberg Richard
Hindon, that she was nothing but a spoiled, pampered darling
who couldn't be got rid of fast enough! Had she even got time
to make him change his mind about her?

PALACE OF THE POMEGRANATE
by Violet Winspear

Life had not been an easy ride for Grace Wilde and she had
every reason to be distrustful of men. Then, in the Persian
desert, she fell into the hands of another man. Kharim Khan,
who was different from any other man she had met . . .

If you have difficulty in obtaining any of these books through
your local paperback retailer, write to:

Mills & Boon Reader Service
P.O. Box 236, Thornton Road, Croydon, Surrey, CR9 3RU.